S0-AQM-101

"Remember our agreement," Adam said. "We want a clean break when the time comes."

"That's what *you* want," Roni said.

Now he frowned openly. Leaning close, he asked, "So what do you want?"

"We made vows, Adam. For better, for worse, through sickness and health. We promised to love, honor and cherish. Then we sealed those vows with a kiss. Did you have your fingers crossed all that time?"

Again she had that odd rush of tears. Again she forced it at bay. Adam would hate it if she showed pity for him.

She dropped her hands to her lap. "Sometimes, life won't let you take a 'time-out' from living," she told him very gently. "We are truly married, whether you want to be or not."

Dear Reader,

It's October, the time of year when crisper temperatures and waning daylight turns our attention to more indoor pursuits— such as reading! And we at Silhouette Special Edition are happy to supply you with the material. We begin with *Marrying Molly,* the next in bestselling author Christine Rimmer's BRAVO FAMILY TIES series. A small-town mayor who swore she'd break the family tradition of becoming a mother *before* she becomes a wife finds herself nonetheless in the very same predicament. And the father-to-be? The very man who's out to get her job....

THE PARKS EMPIRE series continues with Lois Faye Dyer's *The Prince's Bride,* in which a wedding planner called on to plan the wedding of an exotic prince learns that *she's* the bride-to-be! Next, in *The Devil You Know*, Laurie Paige continues her popular SEVEN DEVILS miniseries with the story of a woman determined to turn her marriage of convenience into the real thing. Patricia Kay begins her miniseries THE HATHAWAYS OF MORGAN CREEK, the story of a Texas baking dynasty (that's right, *baking!*), with *Nanny in Hiding,* in which a young mother on the run from her abusive ex seeks shelter in the home of Bryce Hathaway—and finds so much more. In *Wrong Twin, Right Man* by Laurie Campbell, a man who feels he failed his late wife terribly gets another chance to make it up—to her twin sister. At least he *thinks* she's her twin.... And in Wendy Warren's *Making Babies,* a newly divorced woman whose ex-husband denied her the baby she always wanted, finds a willing candidate—in the guilt-ridden lawyer who represented the creep in his divorce!

Enjoy all six of these reads, and come back again next month to see what's up in Silhouette Special Edition.

Take care,

Gail Chasan
Senior Editor

Please address questions and book requests to:
Silhouette Reader Service
U.S.: 3010 Walden Ave., P.O. Box 1325, Buffalo, NY 14269
Canadian: P.O. Box 609, Fort Erie, Ont. L2A 5X3

The Devil You Know

LAURIE PAIGE

SPECIAL EDITION

Published by Silhouette Books

America's Publisher of Contemporary Romance

If you purchased this book without a cover you should be aware that this book is stolen property. It was reported as "unsold and destroyed" to the publisher, and neither the author nor the publisher has received any payment for this "stripped book."

To T., who is serving her country.
Thanks for writing, Laurie.

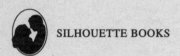 SILHOUETTE BOOKS

ISBN 0-373-24641-2

THE DEVIL YOU KNOW

Copyright © 2004 by Olivia M. Hall

All rights reserved. Except for use in any review, the reproduction or utilization of this work in whole or in part in any form by any electronic, mechanical or other means, now known or hereafter invented, including xerography, photocopying and recording, or in any information storage or retrieval system, is forbidden without the written permission of the editorial office, Silhouette Books, 233 Broadway, New York, NY 10279 U.S.A.

All characters in this book have no existence outside the imagination of the author and have no relation whatsoever to anyone bearing the same name or names. They are not even distantly inspired by any individual known or unknown to the author, and all incidents are pure invention.

This edition published by arrangement with Harlequin Books S.A.

® and TM are trademarks of Harlequin Books S.A., used under license. Trademarks indicated with ® are registered in the United States Patent and Trademark Office, the Canadian Trade Marks Office and in other countries.

Visit Silhouette Books at www.eHarlequin.com

Printed in U.S.A.

Books by Laurie Paige

LAURIE PAIGE

Laurie has been a NASA engineer, a past president of the Romance Writers of America, a mother and a grandmother. She was twice a Romance Writers of America RITA® Award finalist for Best Traditional Romance and has won awards from *Romantic Times* for Best Silhouette Special Edition and Best Silhouette in addition to appearing on the *USA TODAY* bestseller list. Recently resettled in Northern California, Laurie is looking forward to whatever experiences her next novel will send her on.

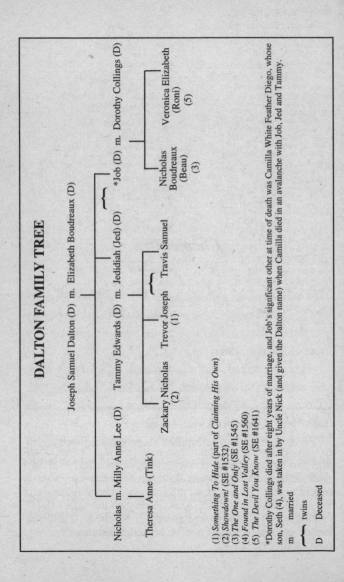

DALTON FAMILY TREE

Joseph Samuel Dalton (D) m. Elizabeth Boudreaux (D)

Nicholas m. Milly Anne Lee (D)   Tammy Edwards (D) m. Jedidiah (Jed) (D)   *Job (D) m. Dorothy Collings (D)

Theresa Anne (Tink)

Zackary Nicholas   Trevor Joseph   Travis Samuel

Nicholas Boudreaux (Beau) (3)   Veronica Elizabeth (Roni) (5)

(1) *Something To Hide* (part of *Claiming His Own*)
(2) *Showdown!* (SE #1532)
(3) *The One and Only* (SE #1545)
(4) *Found in Lost Valley* (SE #1560)
(5) *The Devil You Know* (SE #1641)

*Dorothy Collings died after eight years of marriage, and Job's significant other at time of death was Camilla White Feather Diego, whose son, Seth (4), was taken in by Uncle Nick (and given the Dalton name) when Camilla died in an avalanche with Job, Jed and Tammy.

m married
{ twins
D Deceased

Chapter One

Veronica Dalton glanced at her watch and wrinkled her nose in mock despair. "Gotta punch the time clock," she declared. She counted out enough money to cover her part of the check and tip.

Her best friend, Patricia Upjohn, rolled her eyes at the totally false statement. "Roni, Roni," she scolded. "Count your blessings. Others should be so lucky as to have your hours. And your boss."

With a degree in computer science, Roni worked at home, writing computer learning games for children. Her actual working hours were up to her.

And Patricia was right about the boss. Besides being nice, a great guy and all that, he was a hunk. A woman with any sense would go for him in a heartbeat.

Roni tried to look contrite. "I agree. You bankers pay the price for serving humanity."

"We do our best," Patricia said humbly.

This time it was Roni who rolled her eyes. "Same time next week?" she asked, standing.

"Right."

She bid her friend goodbye and threaded her way through the luncheon crowd. The Friday crunch was getting worse, it seemed to her. They might have to select another day for their weekly lunch. Maybe she could talk her boss into changing their Friday morning meetings to Monday.

No, bad idea. People tended to be grouchy first thing on Mondays. Tuesdays would work, though. Or Wednesdays.

Contemplating what other day of the week would be better for Patricia, she detoured past a group who were still saying their farewells and blocking the narrow space around their table. At that moment, one of the departing men stepped backward without looking. He crashed into Roni, sending her careening to the right…and facedown onto the next table.

At nose level—she wasn't quite lying prone on the white cloth—she observed as water glasses and coffee cups jostled wildly while dinner plates skidded dangerously near the edge. She had a split second to be grateful the plates were mostly empty and that she hadn't landed on one.

The larger and older of the two men took the brunt

of the accident as hot and cold liquids sloshed onto his lap.

"I'm so sorry," she managed to say as the man leaped from his chair and gave her an indignant glare as he brushed droplets from his clothing. Luckily his napkin had absorbed most of the damage.

"Oh, sorry," muttered the coward who'd bumped her. He hurried away, leaving her to face the wrath of the drenched diner alone.

"Use this," a masculine baritone advised.

A clean napkin was thrust into her hand. She carefully blotted drops off the other man's tie. "Blot, don't swipe," she told the furious diner. "That way, you won't push the stain into the material."

Having grown up in an all male household—two older brothers, three older cousins, plus Uncle Nick, who'd raised all six orphans—she'd learned early how to manage most household tasks. Finished, she surveyed the man. "There, not a stain in sight," she said in relief.

"A good thing for you," the man snarled.

"It wasn't her fault," his companion said. "The other man knocked her off her feet. Are you okay?" he asked her.

Roni swung her head around in shock as recognition flashed through her. A jolt went all the way to her toes as she met the cool gray gaze of the man who'd handed her the napkin. "Adam!" she said, then couldn't think of another word, she was that surprised to see him.

Adam Smith was the very attractive but aloof brother of Honey Smith Dalton, who was married to Roni's cousin Zack. Neither had mentioned that Adam was expected in the area. Why was he in the city rather than at the ranch? And why was he dressed in a business suit? Was he working?

Along with the questions came the intense excitement and pure joy of seeing him, all mixed up with a welter of other emotions too confusing to be defined. So she stood there smiling at him, speechless but smiling radiantly in happy surprise.

"Hello, Little Bits," he said with casual amusement.

Before she could question him about his presence in Boise, Idaho, when she knew he worked in the southern California office of the FBI, he stood, gathered her close and kissed the startled "Oh!" off her mouth.

In this swirl of confusion, she felt herself being lifted off her feet and turned so that Adam's back was to his companion. He released her mouth and nibbled at her ear. "I'll explain later," he murmured for her hearing only.

She blinked, forced herself to breathe, then nodded as if she knew what he was talking about.

"Roni, this is Greg Williams," Adam continued, turning them to the other man. "Greg, Veronica Dalton. Call her Roni if you value your life."

Greg was poster handsome, but beginning to run to fat. Too many three-martini lunches, she surmised. He wasn't as old as she'd first thought, but was around the same age as Adam, who was thirty-six, ten years older than her own twenty-six years. Whenever they happened to be at the same place at the same time, he treated her as if she were a precocious six-year-old. Hence her shock at the kiss.

"I didn't realize you had friends here," Greg said to Adam, eyeing them both suspiciously.

"I've worked with her cousin on a couple of things," Adam replied with that same casual amusement. "We met at his wedding. Naturally I looked her up when I came to town."

Liar.

The word leaped to Roni's lips, but she didn't say it. Instead she smiled demurely and tried not to appear confused as the falsehoods fell from his lips as easily as rain from a stormy sky.

His hand rested on the small of her back—a warm, beguiling touch that made her want to lean into him. Since it was totally at odds with the manner in which they'd parted two months ago at her uncle's ranch—he'd made it clear there was nothing between them and there would never be—she resisted the urge.

The only explanation for his sexy, shocking and out-of-character greeting, and his presence here rather than a thousand miles away, was that he must be on a case. Therefore, she would keep her mouth shut and her questions to herself. For the present.

Speculation now leaped into the other man's eyes while he sized her up. He gave a half shrug as if deciding she wasn't his type, then moved aside as the waiter finally came forward and deftly began removing the wet tablecloth.

"See you later," Adam said, his tone affectionate, but the jab in the small of her back told her to leave. Pronto!

She did.

Adam smiled at the friendly squeak of the wooden plank as he crossed the front porch and rang the doorbell of the tiny house located in a block of similar cottage-style homes. The address had surprised him. He'd expected Roni Dalton to live in one of the new, ultrasmart condos being built in prime areas around the city. This neighborhood was definitely blue-collar.

The Saturday morning activities were what he would expect in such a place. It was the third of May, a sunny, pleasant day to be outside. Two doors down, a teenager was polishing an older model car to a high gloss. It was probably his first vehicle. The family compact station wagon was parked on the street.

Next door, an elderly black couple worked in the yard, weeding around hundreds of spring bulbs that were in bloom in raised flower beds. Roni's yard was similar, a springtime riot of flowering quince, forsythia, tulips and daffodils.

For a moment, he recalled that daffodils had been his mother's favorite flower. "Daffy-down-dillies," she'd called them, bringing an armful into the kitchen and arranging them in empty mayonnaise jars so that they'd looked like splashes of sunshine in the house.

An unexpected pang accompanied the nearly forgotten memory, reminding him that once he'd thought life was perfect. Mom and dad, a new baby sister, a house in a quiet neighborhood, flowers and friends and cookouts in the backyard. A ten-year-old's world was small.

The door opened, bringing his thoughts back to the present. Roni gave him an unwelcome glare. "I expected you yesterday," she stated.

She didn't step back and open the door so he could enter. He wasn't inclined to discuss his business on the squeaky wooden porch that ran across the front of the house.

"May I come in?" he asked, keeping his tone neutral and carefully polite. In contrast, his heart was suddenly pumping like an athlete's in the final phase of a triathlon.

She wore a sort of sweat outfit, only it was made of a fleecy material like a baby blanket. Its deep royal blue matched that of her eyes. Dalton eyes. The whole tight-knit clan had those same startling blue eyes, as blue as an afternoon sky on a summer day in the mountains.

Unlike the tall, rangy males in her family, she was petite, maybe five-three, with tiny bones and slender curves. Nearly black hair lay in thick, shining waves to the middle of her back. Black eyebrows and eyelashes accented the color of her eyes and her fair skin. The pink in her cheeks was natural.

A tiny Venus. A tomboy. A computer whiz. He'd met her nearly a year ago and she still intrigued him.

Don't get carried away, he warned, taking an amused

attitude at the heart-pounding, blood-warming sight before him. He'd dealt with women more beautiful, more sophisticated and certainly more agreeable than this one in both his professional and his private life.

However, she could qualify for the most obstinate female he'd ever run across, he decided while he waited for her to make up her mind.

After mulling his request over for a full thirty seconds, she finally moved aside enough so that he could get in the door. Only a tiny part of his mind registered the closing of the door behind them as he surveyed the room.

The place was awash with color, pink and green being predominant. The kitchen and living room had been remodeled into one large, open space with an island separating them. A sink was handily located in the island, and two tall stools on the near side provided a place for casual dining.

On the back wall, an old-fashioned stove, enameled in green, held a simmering pot of soup or stew or something that smelled delicious.

The area rug was green with roses woven into it in multiple hues of pink. A green, white and black border highlighted the center floral part. White beadboard lined the bottom three feet of the wall, matching the cabinets in the kitchen. Pink-striped wallpaper covered the walls of the living room while green and white tiles formed the counter and the backsplash.

An oak armoire was open and revealed a television in its upper section. A sofa in tan and green chenille, an easy chair in tan leather and an oak rocker with pink and green plaid cushions completed a cozy grouping. End tables and a sturdy coffee table were laden with potted plants and magazines about computers and gardening.

The coffee table was painted white, but the green paint from a former life was visible along the edges and legs, and before that, it might have been black. On the walls, family photographs were mixed in casual groupings with gilt-framed mirrors and dark wooden frames of still life paintings that could have come from an ancient attic. Off to one side—where a dining table should have been, he surmised—a quilt was rolled on a quilting frame, a needle with gold thread stuck in one of the squares of material as if the seamstress would be gone only a moment.

The effect of the furnishings was one of odds and ends put together in a charming fashion. For some reason, the place made him feel uneasy, as if he were an unwelcome intruder into her personal space.

"The bathroom is through there," she said, gesturing toward a door.

Adam realized he'd been silent and staring for much longer than polite interest allowed. "What are the other doors?" he asked, indicating the rectangular hallway to the left of the living room. Three doors opened off it, the middle one being the bathroom she'd pointed to.

"Two bedrooms. I use one for an office." She went into the kitchen and held up a coffeepot, giving him a questioning glance.

He nodded, and she poured them each a cup of coffee. She pushed one across the surface of the island in his direction. He stepped closer and leaned an elbow on the green and white tiles while he took a sip of the brew.

"This is good," he said. "Strong and hot, just the way I like it."

"I remember," she said. "From the wedding."

The Dalton family had come to LA so he could participate in his sister's wedding. He'd walked Honey down the aisle and given her into Zack Dalton's loving arms.

The emotion of the moment had surprised him. But then, his little sis was about the only thing in the world that he loved unconditionally and without reserve.

When Honey had been a baby, their father had been killed in a bar shoot-out. The quiet, gentle man hadn't been involved but was just in the wrong place at the wrong moment when a couple of punks had run into each other and pulled their pieces, killing three bystanders. Then their mom had died when Honey was three and he was thirteen. They had gone to live with an aunt who hadn't wanted them.

So much for *his* family ties.

Roni's life hadn't been all that easy, he admitted to himself, pulling out a stool and straddling it. She, too, had been orphaned when a freak avalanche had wiped out her family.

Luckily, her uncle, Nicholas Dalton of Seven Devils Ranch, located near a small town about an hour's drive north of the city, had taken the kids in and given them a good home. A loving home. Yeah, she'd been lucky.

"So what are you doing in town?" she asked, direct and to the point, as usual.

He'd already considered and discarded several answers to this question. He'd decided on the truth. With her, it was the only way. "Working."

"In Boise? Since when?"

Adam smiled in resignation. In a city of barely 200,000 population, he hadn't really thought he could avoid her forever, especially since his sister was married to her cousin. But he'd hoped.

"Since last month. I've been in town two weeks. I'm on new assignment. Bank fraud division."

"Bank fraud," she repeated blankly.

He didn't blame her for the incomprehension. He'd been undercover on a police corruption case when they'd met. The white-collar world of offshore corporations, wired money transfers and fake companies was far from rogue cops, drug-trafficking and extortion.

"I recently finished the course work for a degree in business," he added as if this explained everything.

In a way it did. International crime being what it was, agents proficient in accounting and computer science were more valuable to the bureau on a day-to-day basis than sharpshooters and such.

"And?"

He shrugged. "And I've been assigned to this district to investigate corporate fraud."

"Like, you hack into their computer systems and read their e-mails and see what the executive officers are up to?"

"Hardly," he replied. "Banks are required by law to report movements of large sums of money under certain conditions—"

"Money laundering," she interrupted.

"That might figure into it," he admitted.

"Offshore corporations to hide debt," she continued.

Her beautiful eyes gleamed with interest now. He suppressed a groan. He didn't need her meddling any more than he needed the insistent hunger she induced in him. It echoed through him now, a primal drive that couldn't be denied, although he tried to ignore it.

That kiss in March, when they'd both visited their mutual relatives, had been a mistake, a madness that had buzzed through him and shredded his good intentions, which were to avoid her as much as possible and never, ever so much as touch her hand. So here he was, in her charming home, yesterday's kiss fresh in his mind.

What was that saying? Out of the frying pan and into the fire? Yeah, that was it.

"I can help," she told him. "I'm really good with a computer. We could put a worm in their program—"

"I have plenty of expertise within the department to call on," he informed her coolly. "If I need it."

"Yes, I suppose you do," she said, in as cool a tone as he'd used. She glanced at the wall clock. "It's time for lunch. Do you want to join me? There's plenty."

He knew he shouldn't. Common sense told him to leave and not look back. He should make it clear he wanted her to stay out of his life and his cases. Instead, he nodded.

"That smells incredibly good," he said when she set a brimming bowl in front of him.

"Uncle Nick's specialty." Her smile was warm. "On Saturday, he'd throw all the leftovers in a pot and make 'poor-man's stew.' With fresh bread, that was our dinner."

She removed a big skillet of corn bread from the oven, flipped it over on a platter, cut it into wedges, then put it and the butter on the island. She joined him on the matching stool. "Here's to your health," she said, picking up her spoon.

He ate three pieces of corn bread and two bowls of stew. "That was the best meal I've had since…since I last visited your uncle's ranch."

Instead of looking pleased at the compliment to her relative, her mood became pensive.

"What?" he asked, his voice dropping a register and sounding way too intimate in the silent cottage. He cleared his throat.

"Uncle Nick," she murmured. "Beau says he's doing fine, but I worry about him. He's had a couple of spells with his heart this winter. I wish…"

"You wish?" he finally prompted when she was silent for a long minute.

"I wish we could find Tink for him."

Adam knew that Theresa, or Tink, as she was called,

was Nick's only child and had disappeared at the scene of a car wreck that had killed her mother when the girl was only three and a half. The Dalton patriarch was in his seventies and had always longed to find his missing daughter. Beset with heart problems, his time could be running out.

For a few seconds, he contemplated the older man's pain at losing his wife and child in that manner, then he shook his head. That was one reason he'd never let himself get too deeply involved with a woman. Emotion was too costly.

"What?" he asked, noting Roni's sharp stare.

"Maybe you could help. I know, you can help me find Tink, and I'll help you with your case." She smiled brightly as if this solved some grand problem in the universe.

"Huh," he said, putting a damper on that idea.

She gave him a grimace, then her impish grin returned. "You'll be sorry you turned down such a good offer. I make a hundred dollars an hour as a consultant in my spare time."

"Bully for you," he muttered.

She laughed, then refilled his coffee cup. "Let's go over here where it's more comfortable."

He took the leather easy chair while she snuggled into a corner of the sofa, kicked off her loafers and tucked her feet under her. Heat stirred through him. It settled in the lower part of his body, making him hot and wary of lingering in her house.

His usual reaction to her, he admitted. Lust and caution. How was that for a mixed combination?

"When did you get this place?" he asked as the silence became heavy with tension. Or maybe it was just him.

She seemed perfectly at ease as she blew gently over the surface of the hot coffee. "A month ago. I often jogged through this neighborhood and saw it as soon as it came on the market. I decided I'd rather have a house of my own, so I sold the condo and bought this."

"With the increase in home prices, that was probably a wise move."

"Will you be looking for a place to buy?"

"No."

"You needn't look as if a home is a ball and chain. It could be a good investment, even for someone who moves around fairly often. And you get tax breaks. My brother has preached home ownership as long as I can remember."

Adam assumed she referred to Seth, who was an attorney and the oldest of her siblings. Her other brother was a doctor. One of her cousins was a deputy sheriff—he'd told Greg the truth when he'd said he'd worked with Roni's cousin—while two others were ranchers. The five Dalton males and Roni, the lone female of the six orphans taken in by their uncle, had pitched in to build a resort in the mountains beside a small lake. If all went well, it was supposed to open this summer.

He realized that, with his sister married to the deputy, he knew a lot about the Dalton family. Their ancestors had been on the ranch for well over a hundred years. First Family of Idaho and all that. One cousin was married to a senator's daughter. The senator was running for governor and would likely be elected in November.

For himself, he knew his family history only to his parents. All the grandparents had died before or shortly after his birth. Where their people had come from, he hadn't a clue, except they were European for the most part with a little Hispanic and possibly Native American brought in from his mother's grandmother.

Giving himself a mental shake, he wondered what the heck was wrong with him today. A glance at Roni gave him a hint. Each time he came into contact with her he ended up frustrated and angry.

Because he wanted her.

"What is it?" she suddenly asked.

"What is what?" he countered.

"Heavy sigh. Grim face. I know you aren't involved with a woman. So, did someone just shoot your dog?"

"How do you know I'm not involved with a woman?" he demanded, irked at her certainty.

"Honey said you didn't allow anyone to get too close. Your sister worries about your being all alone in the cold, cruel world."

"My sister should take care of herself and not worry about me," he muttered.

Roni smiled. "Then you know she's expecting."

The news stunned him.

She studied him. "You didn't know. Well, no one

told me it was a secret. She announced it last Sunday when we had dinner at the ranch. If you visited more often, then you would catch up on the news."

A baby. His little sister. He'd looked after her since she was three years old. It felt odd that she was now involved in a major life change with no input from him.

Roni continued, her eyes dreamy the way women's went when talking about babies and all that. "With Beau having a son, then Travis and Alison having their baby in March and now Zack and Honey expecting, Uncle Nick is in heaven. He's hot after the rest of us to settle down and start families."

Other than his sister's nuptials, Adam had avoided the rash of Dalton marriages the past year by dint of his work. Roni's two brothers had married only a few months ago.

"Must be something in the water," he said, irritated by this whole conversation.

The youngest Dalton orphan laughed in delight. "That's what I told Uncle Nick. I said I was bringing my own bottled water with me to the ranch in the future."

"Good thinking," Adam told her sardonically.

She gave him a shrewd glance. "Uncle Nick said if I got pregnant without being married the man would answer to him."

"And to your brothers and cousins."

"Yes. They all agreed they would straighten things out for me."

Her laughter became a sigh as she lapsed into introspection. Women made him nervous when they talked of babies and marriage. He had no time for it, and he always made that clear at the beginning of a relationship.

Relationship? Other than one six-month, on-again, off-again entanglement, at the end of which he'd been accused of indifference, he hadn't seen a woman socially for…mmm, two years?

Yep, it had been at least that long. Once he'd started working on the police corruption case in LA, he'd been in deep cover. He hadn't even communicated with his sister except under the most secret of coded messages.

Even that precaution had failed.

The thugs had sent hit men looking for her in order to flush him out. She could have been killed—

He put a halt to his morbid thoughts. All had ended well with the case wrapped up, the hit men and the bad cops behind bars and his life in the open again. Investigating corporate crime was mostly an office job, nine to five and weekends free.

Free.

That suited him just fine and that was the way he intended to stay. Women always wanted more—more time, more commitment, more of everything. He'd learned to keep things on a light note.

"Anyway," he said, eager to finish the conversation and get out of the cozy bungalow, "I just wanted to let you know I'm too busy to be involved with you in any capacity."

There, that should make things clear to her.

Her dark, delicately arched eyebrows rose as she gave him a lofty perusal.

"Get over yourself," she advised.

Chapter Two

The following Friday Roni surveyed the outfits she'd selected, decided they would have to do, and closed her suitcase. If she hadn't accepted Scott's invitation a month ago to spend a leisurely weekend at the Masterson family estate, she would have preferred to stay home.

Ah well, it might do her good to get out of the house and away from the city for the weekend. After months of near total absorption, she'd finished her part of the current project and turned over the files to her boss that morning.

Reaching a goal usually gave her a lift, but not this time. She was drained mentally and physically, having driven herself to exhaustion the past week to bring the software learning program in on time.

Hearing the doorbell, she quickly slipped into a

denim jacket, glanced around to make sure she wasn't forgetting anything, then grabbed her suitcase and headed for the door.

"Hello. I hope we're ahead of the traffic," she said to the handsome young scion of one of the richest families in the area.

"I'm afraid not. It's already backed up on the freeway. I drove the back streets to get here. It was faster." Scott Masterson smiled, took the luggage and held the screen door while she secured the dead bolt. "Ready?" he said when she turned to him.

"Ready."

His car was a top-of-the-line model. Leather seats. Heated, of course. If she could figure out the buttons on the side of the seat, she thought she could probably get a massage, too. Scott caught her amused smile and smiled back.

He was the country club-tennis set type, with dark hair and eyes, a lean profile, great teeth and smile, charming and polite…everything a maiden's heart could wish for.

Another image came to mind—a stern, forbidding face that somehow had the ability to rock her heart. Adam had appealed to her from the first moment they'd met nearly a year ago. Her cousin Zack had been shot while working on a case with the elusive FBI agent.

She'd also known from the first that Adam was bad news as far as she was concerned. The sparks had been there between them, but he'd stayed aloof. And, as his sister had once said, Adam was like a will-o'-the-wisp, a here today, gone tomorrow type of guy.

The type to break a girl's heart into pieces.

One couldn't say he didn't play fair. He'd warned her there would be no involvement of any kind. He was dedicated to his job. Because of its inherent danger, Adam hadn't allowed close relationships. But that was then, and this was now. Now, he worked in the fraud division, and he'd moved to her territory. Not that this necessarily meant anything, but it was something to think about.

Her attitude lightened as the miles peeled away beneath the tires. The country road ran alongside the Boise River, first on one bank, then across a bridge and on the other side for a while, leisurely tracing the meander of the rushing water farther into the country.

Shortly before five o'clock, Scott turned onto a gravel driveway. The roadside was lush with native trees and flowering shrubs that opened suddenly to allow a view of rolling meadows dotted with cattle, then a lawn and a neotraditional-style house—white, two stories, balcony over a broad, welcoming front porch—nestled into a gentle hill.

"Lovely," she said.

"It's home," he said modestly.

She noted the affection in his tone. He'd grown up here and it obviously meant as much to him as the ranch did to her. Her eyes went misty, surprising her. She wasn't the sentimental sort.

Growing up with five boisterous boys hadn't left

much time for sentiment, she mused wryly as Scott hit a button, waited for the garage door to open, then pulled into the space. She'd learned early in life not to cry. Tears were wasted on men.

Blinking the odd moment of emotion away, she saw that the Masterson garage was neater than her house. In fact, there was nothing but cars in it. No lawn equipment or trash barrels or half-used paint cans.

Yeah, but they have servants, she concluded, excusing her penchant for clutter and familiar things around her.

"This way," Scott said, carrying his weekend case and her larger piece of luggage. He probably had a closet full of clothes here as well as in his condo in town.

They went into a family room or den, then up a flight of steps. His room was next to hers, he told her, indicating a door as he set his case down in front of it. He led the way into the next bedroom. She glanced around while he placed her case on a rack in the spacious closet.

"This is truly lovely," she said.

The room was *très chic,* done in shades of beige and gold. From the off-white, cream and beige tumbled marble tiles in the bathroom to the solid marble panels surrounding the fireplace, from the light beige carpet to the deeper toned satin comforter shot with gold that covered the bed, it was a study in peaceful luxury.

Pillows were heaped on the bed, the smallest covered in gold satin with velvet ribbons, the middle ones in tan, beige and gold stripes and the largest ones covered in pillow shams of golden-brown suede cloth.

Two padded chairs formed an intimate grouping before the fireplace, which was filled with greenery and pinecones and had a many-branched candelabra on the hearth.

A writing table and chair were placed before two tall windows. From the vantage point of the second floor, she could see the tennis courts where a man and woman played against each other with zealous intent to win.

She noted the man had brown hair with golden streaks. The woman was all blond, but Roni thought that was with the help of a good hair stylist. Judging from the similarity in facial features, the woman was Scott's sister. The man's back was to her, so she couldn't identify him. She turned to her host.

"I feel as if I'm in a very exclusive spa," she told Scott after he made sure she had everything she needed.

He grimaced. "My stepmother had all the rooms updated a couple of years ago. It was too Victorian, she said."

His mother had died of breast cancer a few years ago. His father had remarried eight months later. A rush of sympathy made her smile perhaps too warmly. Before she realized what was happening, he'd bent close and kissed her.

"Cocktails at six in the library," he murmured in a definitely husky voice.

After he left, she ran her fingers over her mouth as if wiping the kiss away. She and Scott had hit it off right away when she did some consulting work for CTC-Cascade TelCom, a telecommunications company his grandfather had started—but she wasn't ready for serious involvement.

And his gaze had been very serious.

That worried her. Uncle Nick had lectured them about hurting other people's feelings or letting things go too far when friendship was all you had in mind. He was big on honesty and all that.

Drifting to the double set of windows, she gazed out at the idyllic scene. The sun was going down and the house shaded the two tennis courts. The man served a high-speed ace, which the woman wasn't able to return. She shook her racket at him.

Although she couldn't hear it, Roni could tell the man was laughing. Then the woman was, too. They walked off the court and, chatting animatedly, came toward the house.

Roni's heart gave a lurch she felt throughout her body. It couldn't be! It just couldn't be!

When he looked up as the couple climbed the steps onto the patio, she quickly stepped back from the window.

You can run, but you can't hide.

Her uncle's cautionary advice rang through her head as she glanced around the room as if looking for a bolthole to crawl into. While Uncle Nick meant a person couldn't hide from his or her own conscience, Roni only wanted to hide from the man she would surely have to face when the family gathered for cocktails.

What would Adam think upon seeing her?

And why the heck was she feeling guilty about it?

She hadn't followed him. In fact, if she'd known he was to be here, she would have gone to the ranch or somewhere equally far from this luxurious country estate.

Well, there was only one way to deal with a vindictive fate—meet it head-on and with your best foot forward.

Going to the closet, she removed the long black skirt and black jersey top with brilliant orange and gold poppies embroidered around the neckline. She added fire-coral earrings and tied her hair at the back of her neck with a thin, black ribbon.

She was more careful than usual in putting on makeup. She also decided on the sandals with the two-inch heels rather than the embroidered slippers she had planned to wear for the "at-home" evening. When she put her best foot forward, she wanted to appear as tall as possible.

"Roni, this is my stepmother, Danielle. You've met my father," Scott said, escorting her to the older couple who stood beside a mobile tea cart in the library. "Dad, you remember Roni Dalton, don't you? She was the consultant who wrote the computer program for the company orientation project that was such a success."

Charles Masterson shook hands with her. "Of course I remember. Nice to see you again."

It had been almost three months since she'd completed that task. During the interim she'd seen Scott four or five times for dinner, but not during the past month due to work. After refusing other invitations, she hadn't had the heart to say no to this weekend. Now more than ever she wished she had.

"A computer consultant," Danielle Masterson said. "How interesting. I took several computer courses while studying for my accounting degree and found them fascinating."

Roni managed to keep her mouth from gaping at this statement. She had assumed the woman had been Mr. Masterson's assistant or secretary or something like that.

The woman gave a little laugh. "Did you think I was a social butterfly? I was a financial officer at the company for a year before Charles and I married. That's how we met."

"I see," Roni said, wondering if the woman had gotten her claws into Charles while he was deep in grief over his wife's tragic death.

Maybe she was being unfair. Danielle could obviously make her own way in the world without snagging a rich husband. Although extra money always came in handy, she thought with a cynical attitude new to her.

After she and Scott were supplied with glasses of white and red wine respectively, they moved on.

"This is my sister, Geena," Scott continued, directing her attention to the other couple in the room. "And her guest, Adam Smith."

Roni had spotted him as soon as they entered the library. The smile remained on his mouth, but the look she got from those cool gray eyes told her he wasn't pleased.

She mentally shrugged. He hadn't informed her of his social calendar, so how was she to know he would be here? And why was he?

His sister worried about his love life, or lack thereof, and Roni had flirted outrageously with him over the past year. He'd watched her every maneuver with sardonic amusement and great detachment. Most of the time. There had been that one kiss…

Anyway, she knew he wasn't the kind to get emotionally involved. Unless he'd really fallen for the fair Geena?

The thought was so painful, she had to press a hand against her tummy to stop the tumult. Last Christmas, he'd made it clear by his indifference that he wasn't, and never would be, interested in her. Her New Year's resolution had been to enjoy life and stop daydreaming about one stubborn FBI agent who traveled fast, far and alone.

However, March had come and with it, the kiss, which had burned clear down to her soul and filled her with such dreams, such longing. Her resolve to forget him had gone up in smoke.

He'd left the ranch and she hadn't heard from him until their encounter last Friday. If not for that, she wouldn't have known he was in town.

So be it. Since he was using his real name, she wouldn't have to guard her tongue every moment of the weekend, assuming he was staying until Sunday as she was. Now she waited to see if he acknowledged they knew each other or if they were going to pretend to be strangers.

"Roni and I are old friends," Adam said with casual ease. "In fact, we're almost relatives. My sister is married to her cousin." His smile was all innocent warmth.

"I'm glad to meet you," Roni said to Geena.

She almost laughed at her own earlier vanity in trying to appear taller, as if that might make her more commanding or something. The lovely Geena, wearing three-inch heels, was on level with Adam's six-foot height. Scott was an inch taller than the other two.

As with her family—all the Dalton males tended to be tall and lean—she felt like the odd man, uh, person, out. However, she had learned long ago not to be intimidated by size or any other facet of human differences.

"It is a small world," Geena commented when the group was seated in a pleasant arrangement before the library fireplace. "Adam didn't mention relatives in the city."

"My sister and her husband live in the Hells Canyon area north of here," Adam said.

"So you've known Roni a long time?" the other woman asked.

"Only about a year, actually."

Geena turned to Roni. "Is your brother in finance?"

"He's a deputy sheriff. And he raises and trains cutting horses. Prize cutting horses," she added for no good reason except she wanted this high-class female to know they had some good bloodlines, too, even if it was in the stock they raised.

Again, laughter nearly escaped her before she could sternly clamp down on herself. Geena probably wouldn't be amused at the comparison.

When Adam gave her a narrow-eyed scrutiny, Roni returned it with a wide-eyed innocence, her smile as sweet as molasses taffy. He lofted one thick dark eyebrow sardonically, then turned the conversation to a business topic with Mr. Masterson.

At seven o'clock, they went into the dining room for a dinner that lasted until eight-thirty. The talk around the table ranged from the stock market to politics and the campaigns that were already being waged for elections that were months, or even years, away. Roni mostly listened.

Adam mentioned that another Dalton cousin was married to a woman whose father was running for governor. Drawn into the conversation, she reported that his campaign seemed to be going well and he was ahead in the polls.

After dinner, the two older couples played bridge while she and Scott selected CDs of soft music and chatted quietly. By eleven o'clock she could hardly keep her eyes open.

"We'd better call it a night before Cinderella turns into a pumpkin," Adam said in amusement as she tried to hide another yawn. "The Daltons are an 'early to bed, early to rise' family. I learned that on my first visit to the ranch when Roni woke me up at six in the morning for breakfast. I had agreed to ride out with them on a roundup and a picnic in the mountains for some weird reason I can't recall."

That brought chuckles from the group as the family gazed from Adam to her.

"Scott, show Roni the breakfast room," the stepmother told him. She smiled cordially at Roni. "I'll tell the housekeeper to be sure the coffee is ready by six. Is there anything special you would like to eat?"

"No, cereal or toast is fine," Roni replied.

Geena's smile wasn't quite as friendly when Roni bid them good-night and left the room with Scott at her side. After guiding her to the breakfast room, he led the way up the stairs. She ducked inside her bedroom before he could give her a kiss.

Alone, she dropped the good-natured pose. Curving her fingers into claws, she gave a throaty growl at her image in the mirror over the fireplace, then spoiled the effect by sticking her tongue out at herself.

Fighting a vague sense of despair, she smiled ruefully at her childish display and prepared for bed. Once settled for the night with the lamp off, she found her eyes refused to close or her mind to stop going around and around with fragments of thought. She hoped the weekend would go by fast. Or that Adam would have to leave in the morning.

Next she wondered where he was sleeping…and if he was alone in the bed.

"Arggghhh," she groaned and pulled the pillow over her head as if that would block out the hateful images that sprang into her mental vision.

* * *

In the morning, Roni polished off an English muffin with strawberry preserves, drank the last swallow of milk and wondered what she should do with her dishes.

Adam strolled in, wearing khaki slacks and a chambray shirt with the sleeves rolled up on his forearms. "I thought you would be up."

"Yes. I nearly always wake when the sun comes up."

He nodded as he went to the buffet and looked over the selection of hot and cold foods. Scrambled eggs and bacon were kept warm in a silver double boiler, a smaller version of those she'd seen at hotel buffets. The heat came from a tiny can of fuel of a type she'd used while camping.

The memory of another morning rushed into her mind like the rays of the rising sun that warmed the earth…

She and Adam had leaned on the fence and watched the horses munch hay from a rolled bale. A cool breeze blew down the valley from He-Devil peak. Most of the snow was gone from the pasture due to an unusually warm winter. With the coming of March, the storm pattern had changed, and snow was predicted by Monday, which was only two days away.

"You'd better head south," she'd told him, "before the storm gets here. The county roads will be closed if we get a heavy snow."

"Anxious to get rid of me?" he'd drawled.

She'd hated the amusement in his eyes, the way he had of treating her like a child when she was twenty-six and had been making her own way since graduating from high school.

While Uncle Nick had helped so she hadn't had to go into debt, she'd earned most of her way through college via a work-study program at the education company where she was now employed. She hadn't felt truly young and carefree in years, maybe not since her father had died the winter before she'd turned four.

"Yes," she'd answered. "You bother me in ways I don't like. Because I seem to have no control over myself when you're near."

He sucked in a strangled breath.

She smiled wryly. "That got a reaction out of you."

Suddenly he was close, too close for her comfort range. "Was that all you wanted—to get a reaction from me?" he demanded with an intensity she'd rarely seen in him.

He'd always kept them on a maddening level of casual amusement, as if he silently laughed at the attraction she was sure existed between them.

"No," she said honestly. "No, I want more."

She held her ground with an effort, refusing to look away from the gaze that was no longer cool, no longer amused. A tremor shook her as he came closer.

"Be careful what you wish for," he warned, his voice soft, the tone harsh.

Once she'd wished her mother was alive, that her father would miraculously reappear, that Aunt Milly and Tink would come home, that the other orphans wouldn't move on to high school and college and leave her behind…so many things she'd wished for. None had ever come true.

"I gave up on wishes long ago," she said and heard the echo of sadness in the words. "Except maybe for this."

Then she did a foolish thing. She kissed him.

His arms swept around her and lifted her off her feet. Raising her legs, she wrapped them around his strong masculine frame while her arms encircled his shoulders. She held on as a storm of passion swept over them, through them, as strong in him as it was in her.

It was wonderful and frightening, fulfilling and yet not enough, too many things for her to think about. She quit trying and simply let the hunger take her.

When he slid his hand under her coat, then her sweater, she shivered with delight. His touch was cool at first, but soon warmed as he explored from her neck to her waist, stopping when he touched the top of her jeans.

She pulled back and turned ever so slightly.

It was enough of an invitation. He cupped one hand under her, lifting her onto the rail where cowboys once tied their horses. Now they were at eye level. He slipped both hands under the bulky sweater she wore, caressing upward until he came to her breasts. His thumbs stroked across the tips, which seemed ultrasensitive under the thin barrier of lace she'd worn that morning.

Sensation plunged through her, as wild as a mustang fresh off the range. She hadn't known longing could be like this, or that pleasure could be so strong it bordered on pain. She gasped his name.

He kissed the word from her lips, pulled the breath out of her body with his mouth.

But she didn't need air now, only his touch. She was all dancing flames, burning wild and out of control across the windy plain that was her soul. Her heart was engulfed in the magic of his fiery embrace.

And then he was gone.

She stared in confusion as he pivoted and turned his back to her. "Adam?"

From six feet away, he faced her, his expression so grim, so filled with disgust, her heart felt as if it had been turned into ice.

"I'm sorry," he said. "That shouldn't have happened. I never meant to let it go that far."

"It was wonderful. Why should you be sorry?"

"Because I can't afford to get involved with you."

She smiled because it was obviously too late to worry about that.

He shook his head, fury in his eyes. "Because when it was over, we would still have relatives who are married to each other and that could be awkward."

"Why should it be over?" she challenged. "Maybe we'll fall madly in love, marry and live happily ever after."

"It won't happen," he said, as if he had a crystal ball. "My work is dangerous. I can't afford to lose my concentration by worrying about a family."

"I see," she said, forcing a quietness into her manner that she was far from feeling. She'd learned long ago that men responded to calm and withdrew from tears.

"There's an attraction, a strong one," he admitted, "but that's as far as it goes. I'm not in love with you, and I'm not going to be."

His words echoed inside her where she felt as hollow as a cave. "You've made yourself perfectly clear."

Too proud to let him see the hurt, she smiled, jumped down from the railing and walked into the ranch house.

Hearing her uncle Nick in the kitchen, she stayed in her room until she was totally composed, then she went to help him with breakfast. The next morning Adam was gone when she rose. His sister's lack of surprise later that day told Roni he'd explained his plans to Honey, but not to her.

Only her older brother had known of her feelings. Seth would keep a secret to the grave, so she didn't have to fear pitying glances from the rest of the family.

For the present, she only had to get through the rest of this weekend, then she could go home and privately lick the wounds that hadn't quite healed.

Observing Adam as he set his plate on the table and took the seat opposite her, she wondered at the madness that had seized them both that day. March madness, she thought, recalling Alice and her trip through Wonderland.

"What's funny?" Adam asked, shaking pepper generously over his scrambled eggs.

Her whimsical smile grew. "I was wondering what

it is about March that makes rabbits go mad." At his quizzical glance, she added, "Don't you remember the saying—mad as a March hare?"

He replaced the pepper shaker on the table with a thump. "I was wondering when you would bring that up."

"I wasn't referring to us."

"Like hell you weren't."

She returned his glare, her stubborn nature coming to her rescue. At that moment she wanted to drive him mad with frustration as he tried to figure her out but couldn't.

She hoped.

He caught her wrist. Surprised, she let him take her pulse, which was now pounding in her head. She counted the beats as he did. Dropping her hand, he picked up his knife.

"What's your diagnosis, doctor?" she inquired.

His smile was challenging. "Fast and sassy."

She raised her eyebrows at that. "I have a sassy pulse?"

He looked up from buttering a muffin. "You have a sassy mouth," he said, his voice dropping to a deeper note. "And a sharp tongue that could very well get you into trouble one day. Your relatives should have warned you about that."

She had to laugh. "Well, actually, they have. Many times. Many, many times," she said truthfully.

After a second, he laughed, too.

Now that he was in better humor, there was something she needed to know. She leaned toward him and spoke in a near whisper. "Are you here socially, or are you on a case?"

He was silent so long she thought he wasn't going to answer. Finally he gave a sardonic half smile. "Since you know the family, I suppose you'll ferret out my secrets before the weekend is over. I'm on a case."

She ignored the relief she felt at this information. "Uh, what should I know about you? Do you have a cover?"

"I'm in the equipment leasing business and may be doing some work with their company. This is a relatively new endeavor for me, so you don't know anything about it."

"I'll follow your lead," she promised.

He gave a frankly amused snort.

On that cheerful note, Geena entered the room. She wore white slacks and a white silk shirt with turquoise stones around her neck and dangling from her earrings. Her summer-blond hair was sleek and held back from her face with a black band. She looked like a princess.

After daintily covering a yawn, she glanced at the couple with a smile. "You two are in good humor this morning."

"Join us," Adam invited, rising and holding a chair for her. "Coffee?"

"Please."

He brought her a steaming cup of the delicious gourmet blend, then inquired about her preferences in food.

Roni tried not to get angry about his attentiveness as he served Geena the single slice of toast she'd requested and placed the container of marmalade close at hand.

"My, aren't we the gentleman this morning?" she said and immediately regretted the acid drip on her tongue.

"I've always found Adam to be perfectly charming." Geena smiled into Adam's eyes, her sexy perusal meant for him alone.

Roni experienced the uncomfortable feeling a person got when with others who obviously would have preferred that she disappear so they could have privacy.

Her chin went up. She gazed out at the lawn. "Are you two going to play tennis this morning?"

"I thought we would go for a walk by the river. There are some beautiful rose arbors on the estate." She glanced at Roni. "You might enjoy them, too."

"No, thanks. Roses make me sneeze."

Adam frowned at that, but Roni didn't change her story. He was probably recalling all the flowers in her yard. Well, she did take allergy pills when ragweed was in season. At any rate, Scott was her host. She would wait for him.

Thirty minutes later, the couple left her at the table. She watched them cross the tennis court and stroll down the sloping lawn. Geena slipped her hand into the crook of his arm before they disappeared among the trees that lined the river.

At nine, Mr. Masterson appeared, gulped down a cup

of coffee, then headed out for a golf game. He told her his wife took breakfast in her room and answered her mail in the mornings, that his son didn't usually get up before ten on the weekend and that she should feel free to watch television, read or do whatever she wished until they all met for lunch at one at the country club.

He was a nice man, she reflected after he left. Going to the other room, she read financial magazines until Scott appeared. "Shall we see if we can catch up with the other two?" he asked, bringing a muffin and glass of orange juice to the library with him.

"Sure."

They headed for the river as soon as he finished. There they found Adam and Geena sitting on a bench beneath a bower of white roses. They were just about to kiss, or so it seemed to Roni.

"Hey," Scott said, not at all embarrassed at coming upon the other couple. "Knock it off, you two. It's too early for that sort of thing."

The older couple laughed as they leisurely drew back. Roni indicated the stain on Adam's jaw near his mouth. "Is that your favorite shade of lipstick for day-time wear?" she teased, hiding an unwarranted posses-siveness. Adam wasn't hers. And never would be, according to him.

His eyes met hers. For a second she thought she saw regret in those gray depths and something that seemed warm and sensual and concerned. Then the impression was gone.

He might be here on a case, but that didn't mean his reactions to Geena weren't sincere. The thought hurt, but she had to face it. The other woman was lovely, smart and sophisticated. Why wouldn't Adam be attracted to her?

He wiped his hand across his face and glanced at the resultant smear. "Yes, I think it is." His grin at Geena was sexy and intimate.

Geena removed a tissue from her pocket and gently wiped the color away. "There," she said. "Now we won't embarrass our young guest."

Roni rejected the comparison to a child coming upon a grown-up game she didn't understand. She understood all too well. The other woman was marking her territory.

Chapter Three

After a morning of hiking around the beautiful estate, Adam showered and dressed in fresh khakis and a white polo shirt for the planned luncheon at the country club. He gave a silent whistle upon meeting Geena in the library.

"Very nice," he murmured, ignoring the slight pout to her lips that indicated she would like a kiss. Maybe the weekend visit hadn't been so smart, although it was part of the plan that he should distract the daughter of the house while Greg got Mr. Masterson's approval for the bogus leasing agreements with the fake company Adam represented.

Since Geena knew he was with the FBI and had helped him set up the sting operation, he thought she was taking the friendly pretense a bit far. He hoped she wasn't making plans for the two of them for when the case was resolved.

"Thank you, sir," she said demurely, then laughed.

She wore white slacks with tiny gold stripes and a golden-colored, clingy blouse that crossed over her breasts and tied in the back at her waist. An enticing bit of tanned flesh was visible at her waist. Her gold sandals had three-inch heels, putting her at eye level with him.

He'd always liked his women tall and elegant, he grimly reminded himself. Until he'd met a certain small tomboyish woman who'd shown him the sweetest passion he'd ever known.

Hearing voices from the stairs, Geena picked up her purse, extracted her sunglasses and glanced impatiently toward the corridor. "Are you two ready?" she asked.

Scott and Roni entered the room. Her brother checked the clock. "Yes, we're right on time."

Adam noted the not quite concealed irritation in the other man. Scott and Geena, like many brothers and sisters, didn't get along all that well.

Had circumstances been different, he and Honey might have been at odds, but with the difference in their ages and the fact that they'd had only each other while growing up, they were close. He suddenly missed her.

He wanted to question her about falling in love, about taking a chance on another person, about trusting in luck for once and a gut feeling that he should take what life offered and run with it.

Then what? What came next? Marriage and happily ever after, as Roni so confidently proclaimed?

Upon this odd note, he let himself look at Roni. His heart started pounding, as it had last week at her cottage.

She wore a short white skirt and a formfitting white top with blue sleeves and collar. Like Geena, the top and bottom didn't quite meet, exposing a midsection of smooth flesh. A gold ring with a tiny cross dangling from it pierced the edge of her navel.

His lungs stopped working.

He stared at the bit of gold as it shifted constantly with each movement, each breath she took. He thought of kissing her there, of stripping the skirt from her perfect form and tasting the delectable flesh—

He broke the thought and held his arm out to Geena. "Shall we go?"

They followed the other couple to Scott's car. He forced himself to think of winter snow and icy dips in the river until the fever left his blood.

On the short trip to the country club, he was mostly silent while the two women chatted. Anger—with himself for his lack of control, with his job for bringing him to this place and with the unfairness of life for making him long for things he couldn't have—burned in the pit of his stomach. As soon as he finished the current task, he would request a transfer back to LA.

Fat chance, some snide part of him whispered. The division manager had wanted him out of the LA area after they broke that case so he'd be safe from vengeful cops.

Safe?

Glancing at Roni's dark, gleaming hair in the front seat, he experienced a sinking sensation. He could have gone to New Mexico on a drug smuggling bust. Why had he chosen to come here?

"You're quiet," Geena murmured, leaning close. "Deep, dark thoughts?"

"Very deep, very dark," he said with a wicked smile.

She shivered delicately. "Mmm, sounds delicious."

When she laid a possessive hand on his knee, he didn't pull away. Instead he clasped it in his and held it as they pulled into a parking space at the club. Through the side mirror, he met Roni's eyes. They watched each other for a second as if sizing up an opponent, then she looked away.

He felt as if he'd taken a cheap shot at her. He quickly got out and went around to Geena's side to open her door. Damn, but it was going to be a long weekend.

Halfway through lunch Roni was relieved to see Patricia on the last hole of the golfing green. When her friend finished the game, she stripped off her gloves, spotted Roni and her group, waved madly, then came over. Roni had told her to look for them.

The three men stood.

"Please, gentlemen, keep your seats," Patricia told them. "I just stopped to say hello to Roni. We were roommates in college. She got me through those awful computer courses."

"Patricia corrected all my English papers before I turned them in, or else I would still be trying to graduate," Roni said, returning the implied compliment.

Adam invited Patricia to take his chair and pulled another over from an empty table. The day was sunny, so they had opted to sit on the dining terrace. Roni introduced her friend to the Masterson family and to Adam.

"Upjohn?" Charles repeated the last name. "There's a Thomas Upjohn who lives in the area."

Patricia wrinkled her nose prettily. "My father. I work in the loan department at the bank. Since he has no son, he's decided I need to learn the family business."

"She's a whiz at it," Roni said loyally. "She arranged the loan for my house and got me through all the paperwork. Even Seth approved of the transaction."

She had to explain Seth was her brother and an attorney and that he reviewed all the family legal affairs.

"I know him," the older Masterson told her. "He brought a suit against my company for a client and won. It was a business matter," he added with a smile. "No hard feelings."

Roni nodded.

Patricia ordered a glass of iced tea when the waiter came over, then settled in to chat with them. Roni felt more at ease with her friend there. She'd been to the country club with Patricia on other occasions, and it was nice to have reinforcements, so to speak.

Not that everything wasn't just fine, at least as far as she was concerned, she mused when attention shifted away from her. There was tension between Scott and Geena. She thought the brother and sister didn't like each other very much. Geena had probably bossed Scott around when they were kids, the same as her brothers and cousins had always tried to do to her.

She'd hated being ordered about. Except by Uncle Nick, of course. He was the undisputed boss of the Dalton gang.

Her heart warmed as she thought of the relative who'd taken the orphans in and given them shelter and a loving home. That aspect of him had never changed, not even when his own heart was aching with the loss of his wife and child not quite a year after the orphans had come to live with him and Aunt Milly and Tink.

With only a few months difference in their ages, she and Tink had become fast friends. It had been so nice to have another girl to play with. Then Tink was gone, leaving another hole in her heart...

She realized the others were looking at her. "I'm sorry. What was the question?"

"Shall I see if we can get a tee time for this afternoon?" Geena asked. "There may be a cancellation."

"I don't play golf, but you three go ahead."

"We don't mind helping you," Geena offered graciously. "It's easy to learn."

Roni grimaced to herself. It looked as if she was going to have to join them.

"Actually," Patricia spoke up, "Roni has played a

few rounds with me. She's not bad for a beginner, but watch out for her wicked slice."

Roni couldn't recall if a slice meant she hit the ball to the right while a hook went to the left or vice versa.

Geena rose. "Then it's settled. I'll check with the pro and see if we can get a slot."

Roni had a feeling she wasn't going to enjoy this game at all. "When did you learn to play?" she asked Adam.

"I used to caddy when I was in high school. Sometimes I was asked to fill out a foursome."

"I see."

Charles and Danielle apologized and left them shortly after that. Patricia gave Roni's arm a squeeze and said she had to run. She was in charge of a political dinner that evening for her father, for whom she often served as hostess.

Growing up without a mother had been an immediate bond between the two girls when they'd shared a room their freshman year at school, then an apartment thereafter. Patricia came from a wealthy banking family, but she was friendly and candid and casual about her background.

Scott saw a friend and excused himself, leaving her and Adam at the table. Roni sipped iced tea and observed the next group of golfers at the eighteenth hole.

"Scared?" Adam said.

"Of what?"

He shrugged. "Of looking like an amateur on the golf course. You Daltons don't like to lose."

"Well, I hate to have Geena show me up," she admitted, bringing an unexpected smile to his face, "but I'll live through it."

"Good."

A funny feeling invaded the pit of her stomach at his approving nod. "Uncle Nick said we should try new things as long as it wasn't drugs or something illegal. Geena is probably an expert," she added a trifle glumly.

His smile became a chuckle. "Probably. Just relax and try to enjoy it. Don't worry about the score."

"That's easy for you to say." She sighed loudly. "The grounds are nice here. If nothing else, I can admire the landscape while I'm hacking my way down the fairway."

"Right."

Her attitude lightened as he laughed again. Maybe she would get through this with her dignity intact. She vowed to do her best.

When Geena returned and reported they were scheduled for four o'clock, the problem of shoes came up. Determined not to be outdone by the other woman, Roni bought a pair of golfing shoes at the club. She carefully concealed her shock at the sticker price and put the cost on her credit card. She hoped Uncle Nick didn't find out what she'd paid for them.

"They'll last a long time," Adam said, falling into step beside her as they went to the car where Scott waited.

"They'd better," she said wryly.

Geena, on the other side of Adam, looked amused. "You can play in sneakers, too. Some people do."

Her tone implied that those who did were social wash-outs. Roni smiled brightly. "It's time I learned to play. Patricia loves it and is always after me to join her. Maybe I'll get good enough to show her up."

"What's her handicap?" Geena wanted to know.

Roni hadn't the foggiest idea. "Five."

Geena looked surprised, then dubious.

"Maybe six," Roni said, trying to look as if she knew what she was talking about.

"We'll have to invite her to play sometime," the other woman decided, a competitive light in her eyes.

Roni had thought Patricia was a wonderful player, but now she hoped her friend was pro material. She wanted to see someone beat the socks off the cool blonde, who seemed perfection personified. Maybe someday *she* would beat her, Roni mused, wondering how much golf lessons cost.

Glancing at Adam, who observed them with a slight frown on his handsome face, she hoped he didn't realize she was seething from something very akin to jealousy. She didn't like the feeling at all.

Roni lined up the borrowed driver behind the ball, eyed the flag on the pole at the last hole, then gave it her all. She observed as the ball went shooting off into the rough, hit, then, to her surprise, rolled onto the green. The far edge of the green, yes, but *on* the green, and this was only her second shot.

Geena—the cool, the skillful, the beautiful—drove

straight down the fairway and landed in the middle of the green. Scott and Adam followed, then the foursome climbed in the golf cart and went to play the eighteenth hole.

Geena had played beyond her game, or so she said, and had given Adam a run for his money on the lovely course, coming in only two points behind him. Scott was ten points behind and obviously disgruntled about it. He was probably off his game due to having to play after her.

Her own score was so terrible, Roni saw no need to add it up. She'd lost two balls in the trees and two in water traps. Three times she'd had to pick up and move on without getting the stupid ball in the hole because other people were waiting for the green.

Adam's handicap was nineteen. A handicap less than ten was considered close to pro status, so Geena had known that Roni had been talking through her hat when she'd claimed Patricia was in the five to six range.

Nothing like making a fool of oneself. She hadn't been so humiliated since first grade when she'd forgotten the lines to the poem she'd written for Uncle Nick and he'd been in the audience to witness her failure.

"This is a difficult green," Geena announced.

"Tell me about it," Roni muttered.

Since she was the farthest from the hole, she walked to the edge of the green, stood at a tilt because the rough slanted downward there and, hardly glancing at the hole, gave the ball a whack with the putter Adam handed her.

Three more whacks and she was done, even if she missed every time, she consoled her bruised ego.

The ball rolled merrily with the slope of the green. It was going to miss the hole. She pasted her cheeriest smile on her face. Stoic was her middle name.

Just then the ball swerved to the right. In a long graceful arc, it spiraled over the short grass in a tightening circle. To her amazement, it disappeared.

"A birdie," Geena said. "I don't believe it."

Roni couldn't believe it, either. She walked over to the hole and peered inside. The ball was there.

"Good going," Adam said when she lifted it out of the cup. His eyes were filled with laughter.

She grinned at him, her world right once more. On this buoyant note, Roni made it through the casual dinner and the teasing she took over her score that evening.

During the evening meal, listening to Adam talk business with the Mastersons, she picked up on the fact that the family thought Adam was in some kind of communications leasing business, just as he'd said at breakfast. She also learned that Greg Williams was the chief financial officer of their company.

With a sudden sense of horror, it occurred to her that she might have blown Adam's cover on his current case. She had to speak to him. Right away.

Roni paced the floor. Finally, at half past eleven, she heard Geena's voice, then Adam's, as they ascended the stairs. She eased her door open ever so little and noted which rooms they entered. As she'd suspected, their rooms were side by side, across the hall from hers and Scott's.

At midnight, she figured everyone was in bed and asleep. Except Adam. She could see a sliver of light under his door. She tiptoed across the hall and silently turned the knob.

Adam, dressed in a sweat suit, sat in an easy chair, his feet on the matching ottoman, a book open on his lap. His eyes met hers, their frosty hue not very welcoming.

She slipped inside and closed the door. "I need to talk to you," she whispered.

He nodded, but didn't get up. His gaze swept over her satin pajamas, which were dark blue with a paisley print border in gold on the sleeves and legs.

Going to him, she perched on the edge of the ottoman and leaned close. "You remember a week ago Friday I was at the restaurant with Patricia and you were with—"

"Greg Williams," Adam interrupted rather impatiently.

"Yes, well, you told him you and my cousin had worked on a couple of projects and that we had met at his wedding. Remember?"

He nodded.

"Then last night you mentioned Zack and Honey. I told Geena my cousin was a deputy sheriff—"

"Ah, yes, when you were comparing bloodlines."

She flushed at the sarcastic tone and wished she

hadn't let her baser emotions get the better of her. "I don't think Geena caught on," she said contritely.

"Would it have mattered to you if she had?"

Roni peered into his unfriendly gaze. "Not then," she admitted, "but now I'm truly sorry. I was envious, just for a moment, of all she had."

The silence was brief, but intense.

"What, Little Bits, does she have that you haven't got, tenfold?"

His voice was still stern, but other emotions—tenderness? sympathy? concern?—flicked through his eyes and were quickly hidden. She wondered if they were for her or for the confident Geena.

"Golfing skills," she lamented.

He smiled slightly, and the tension eased. She grinned, then became serious. "Anyway, Mr. Masterson mentioned Greg Williams was with CTC," she said in a barely audible voice.

"What bothers you about that?" Adam asked.

"I may have blown your cover." She pinched pleats into the satin material of her pajamas while she considered the ramifications. "If Geena knows my cousin is a cop and Greg knows you've worked with him and they get to talking and all this comes out, then they may suspect you're a cop."

"I see."

She stared at her nervous fingers and forced them to stop creasing the material. "I feel just wretched."

His low laughter brought her head up. "I knew I was

in for trouble when you fell on my table that day like a warning from heaven. I don't know how I thought I could avoid you." He laughed again. "Or your meddling."

His resigned exasperation hurt, but she had no time for self-pity at the present. "Are you making fun of me?" she demanded. It certainly didn't seem as if he was taking her all that seriously.

"No," he denied, but he was smiling. "Next time you see Greg, flirt with him. Maybe he'll tell you what he's up to."

"Is he cooking the books?"

"He seems to be the brain behind a kiting scheme with an offshore bank as well as various fake contracts. The last company he was with went bankrupt."

"Ah-ha!" She thought furiously. "We really could put a worm in his computer and trace everything he does."

"I know."

"We also need to see who else he's working with in the company. His e-mails could tell us that."

"Right."

His expression had become amused, albeit long-suffering, as she listed the things they could do. She realized he was letting her run on until she ran out of steam and shut up. She managed a smile. "Sorry. I do tend to get carried away. If I ever run into Greg again, what is your relationship with him?"

"I'm advising him on setting up long-term leasing contracts for CTC."

Before leaving, she laid a hand on his arm. "Be careful," she implored huskily. "It's a dangerous game you play. There could be others involved."

"Such as Geena?"

He was teasing, but Roni nodded. "She and Scott work there, and it wouldn't be the first time a man's heirs have sabotaged the family business."

Before he could reply, they heard Geena's voice. "Adam, are you awake?" she called softly.

Roni realized there was a connecting door between the rooms. For a second, she was consumed with anger. "Sorry, I didn't know I was keeping you from a date," she whispered, then dived behind the curtain next to the armoire as the knob rattled, then turned and the door opened.

"Can we talk?" Geena asked, coming into the room.

Through the silk material of the drapes, Roni could see the other woman's outline against the lamp. Geena sat on the ottoman where Roni had perched.

"I saw you talking to my father before dinner. Do you think he suspects anything?"

"No," Adam told the other woman.

"You've been at the office for two weeks. What do you think?"

His soft laughter was amused. "That it's late and we should be thinking about sleep."

Geena also laughed. "I can think of things other than sleep."

Her tone was so suggestive, only a complete idiot could fail to get her meaning. Roni set her teeth and waited to see how Adam would get out of this one. Even the bold FBI agent wouldn't make love to one woman while another hid behind the curtains and observed.

But she wasn't so sure when the shadowy figures merged into one. Geena sighed contentedly and loudly as she settled into his lap. Roni clenched her hands and stilled the indignant pound of her heart.

"What is it?" Geena asked. "You seem tense."

"I'm wondering what to say if your father comes bursting in," Adam told her.

The husky laughter was an open invitation. "Darling, I'm not a schoolgirl. In fact, I was married briefly when I got out of college."

"What happened?"

"I discovered I didn't need another superior male telling me what to do. My father was quite enough."

"We men haven't adjusted to you modern women," Adam commented. "We're still in the caveman era."

Geena's voice became a purr. "There are moments when a woman likes a strong, masterful man."

Their heads merged into one blob against the lighter color of the damask chair. Roni stuck her head out the side of the curtain. Adam gave her a glare while Geena snuggled her head against his throat.

Roni glared back, then ducked behind the curtain again. She'd just wanted to remind him that she was still here.

"Mmm," Geena crooned.

Roni adjusted the curtain so she could see through a gap between it and the armoire. Geena's hand was stroking up and down Adam's chest. He caught it and held it pressed to his chest. His face looked like a thundercloud ready to discharge the lightning that had gathered in it.

"Are you really sleepy?" Geena asked, leaning her head back on his arm. "Adam? What is it? You look…"

Roni waited to hear what word Geena would use to describe his expression, but the other woman shrugged as if she couldn't think of the appropriate term.

"I have a headache," he muttered.

"A headache," Geena repeated as if she'd never heard of such a thing. "Perhaps we can kiss it all better."

Roni had to smile. She was willing to bet the lovely blonde hadn't heard many men claim a headache while she was bent on seducing them. Would Adam have succumbed had he and the temptress been alone? The smile evaporated.

The curtain huffed out as she sighed and brought her temper under control. One thing about having five male relatives around to keep a person straight—she'd learned to take it on the chin, as Seth had often told her she must.

Glancing at the embracing couple, she caught Adam's warning frown. He must have heard the sigh. Oh, well.

"I think it's time to call it a day," he said to his clinging companion.

"Good idea," she murmured, not taking the hint.

He stood and dropped her gently so that she had to stand on her own. "I'll see you in the morning."

With hands on her shoulders, he ushered her from the

room, then flicked the lock after he closed the connecting door. He turned, put a hand to his head as if an ache really had settled there and returned to the chair.

"That was too close for comfort," he muttered.

Roni took a seat on the ottoman again, then crossed her legs and tucked her feet under her. With elbows on her knees, she went over the details of the case.

"Do you think any of the family are in on the scam with Greg Williams?" she asked.

"Why do you ask?"

"Well, Geena is pretty sharp. So is the stepmother, Danielle. And Scott has worked for his father since he was old enough to run a copy machine. Maybe Mr. Masterson doesn't appreciate their work and pays them accordingly. Maybe they want more money, and they want it now."

"Maybe."

"The company stock skyrocketed after Danielle came to work. I remember because my brother made us all buy shares, then he made us sell when the price doubled. When the tech bubble burst, the company lost thirty percent of its value."

"Some tech companies lost ninety percent. Look, could we discuss this another time, like daybreak or something?"

"Do you really have a headache?" she inquired. "I have some pills in my purse—"

He'd been resting with his head against the back of the chair. Now he leaned forward and caught her by the shoulders. "Pills won't help where I ache," he muttered, his face looking like a thundercloud once more.

"Where is it?" she asked in perfect innocence, worried because men never admitted to pain unless it was serious.

He said a curse word, then his mouth was on hers, hot and angry and demanding, then, all at once, gentle and sweet and cajoling.

She couldn't help it. She melted into him.

His arms came around her and lifted her from the footstool. She landed in his lap, her body blending with his in a wonderfully comfortable fit, her hips snug in the groove between his thighs.

His hands searched for the hem of her pajama top, then they were on her skin, gliding up and down her side before he pressed her against his arm and one hand explored her thoroughly, back and front.

He cursed again, then resumed the kiss. Hunger, painful and sharp, arced through her. When he cupped her breast, she pushed against his palm, wanting his touch, needing it with a desperation that only he summoned in her.

Finally she had to turn her head in order to get a breath. He deftly flipped open the buttons between them, then his mouth followed where his hands had been, his tongue skimming over her flesh, pulling in tender sucking motions until sensation ran from the point he touched to all parts of her body.

"It's like being on fire," she whispered.

"I know."

She pressed her forehead against his when he looked up and met her eyes. "I want more."

He closed his eyes as if in pain. "Don't. Don't tempt me," he said in a hoarse voice she'd never heard from him.

Smoothing his hair with fingers that trembled, she admitted, "I want to. I want to drive you mad with longing…the way you do me. For weeks after we kissed at the ranch, I couldn't sleep. I wanted you with me. I ached. For you, only for you."

"Damn, damn, damn," he said softly, a litany of need in the word as he sought control.

"I don't want to stop," she said.

He caught her hands with one of his and held them behind her while he fastened the satin-covered buttons. "Nothing good can come of this, so let's not start."

She wanted to argue, but he looked so tormented, she simply nodded. He stood and placed her on her feet. At the door, he leaned close and said, "Geena was the one who called me on this case. She was the one who thought Greg's financial proposals were suspicious."

With that, he ushered her into the hall and closed the door firmly against the questions that sprang to her mind. She heard the soft click as he locked it.

In her elegant bedroom a few minutes later, she lay in the middle of the huge mattress and went over all that had happened that day.

So. She'd wanted to believe that Geena was working

with Greg, but she'd been wrong. She mentally apologized to the other woman for her ill thoughts.

Rethinking the final few moments in Adam's room, she shivered as the yearning returned. He shared it, but he didn't want to.

She'd had enough of fun and frolic at Scott's family home. In the morning she would ask to go home.

You can run, but you can't hide.

Maybe she was running, but she wasn't hiding, she told her conscience. She knew that Adam didn't want her, not in any way that truly mattered.

Chapter Four

Roni woke before six. Yawning, she climbed out of bed and realized she was still tired. Or maybe she was just crabby. Body and soul, she felt out of sorts, something that wasn't usual with her. She was a morning person and generally bounced out of bed, ready to face the day, fight dragons or whatever presented itself. But not today.

After dressing in shorts, T-shirt and sneakers, she slipped quietly into the hall. She glanced at Adam's door, then away. For the first time in her life, she experienced the acid taste of personal defeat, as if she'd failed at some goal that would decide the direction of her life for all time to come.

In the breakfast room, the Sunday paper was on the sideboard. She ate a serving of scrambled eggs and whole wheat toast, then sipped coffee and watched the weather report on a small television set that had been turned on, its sound muted.

The house was so silent, she felt utterly alone.

Thirty minutes later she left the pleasant room and headed for the path by the river. A good run would clear her head and help get her equilibrium back.

The morning air was cool when she started out, but by the time she'd gone a mile, she was perspiring. She did her usual two miles, then walked another ten minutes before reversing her direction and heading for the house.

She hoped Scott would be up by now so she could ask him to take her home.

Hearing someone running along the path, she stepped aside as Adam rounded the curve. He nodded and swept on by her. She murmured, "Good morning," and kept walking.

A quarter mile from the house, she heard his return. This time when she moved over, he fell into step beside her and wiped his face on a towel hanging around his neck.

"It's going to be warm today," he said.

"In the high seventies, according to the news."

"Yeah."

They walked in silence for another moment.

"Look," he said, his tone grimmer than she'd ever heard, "I'm sorry about last night."

She tried for a teasing manner. "For making out with Geena while I hid behind the curtain?"

"No. For what happened between us."

"Well," she said philosophically, "not much did. You always quit just when things get interesting."

He gave her an exasperated glance, then his face softened. "Look, Little Bits—"

"Don't call me that. I'm twenty-six. That's an adult by anyone's standards," she told him. "Say whatever you have to say so we can be done with this conversation, okay?"

"Fine. Nothing can come of the attraction between us."

She sucked in a sharp breath at his bluntness. She was also aware that he'd actually admitted the attraction was mutual. "Why not?" She really was curious about his reasons.

He wiped the beads of sweat from his face and neck. A bitterness she hadn't expected crept into his face.

"One, cops have one of the highest divorce rates of any profession," he said. "Two, they get killed."

"Your father was killed, and he wasn't a cop," she pointed out. "Life happens."

She wished she hadn't brought up his father. For a second there was the starkest expression on his face—a pain so deep, it caused her to ache, too. Then it was gone.

"He was the kindest, gentlest man I've ever known," Adam said in a low, hoarse voice. "A quiet man who taught himself to play the guitar. He loved music. At night, after I was in bed, I'd hear him sing ballads to my mother. He was gunned down by a couple of punks for no reason. My mother never got over the loss."

"That was the reason you went into law enforcement," she said with sudden insight.

He sucked in a deep breath as if closing the door on memories too precious to share. She knew the feeling. People didn't think she'd been old enough to remember the rodeo days with her father and uncle, the excitement of the crowds, the fun of being with the other kids, but she did.

Happiness. She knew how fleeting it could be.

So did Adam. Perhaps that was why she'd been drawn to him from the first. Instinctively she'd known they were kindred souls.

"I've seen what happens to families when they're separated, either by death or divorce," he continued. "You know how hard it is for kids whose lives are disrupted."

"Yes," Roni agreed, "it's tough. But we survived. So did you and Honey."

"Yeah, but not everyone is lucky enough to have an uncle Nick," he said, returning to his usual sardonic tone. "Besides, I've discovered from personal experience that women aren't good at waiting. They want a nine-to-five kind of man."

"Isn't that what you are now?"

"I'm involved in a sting. People can get hurt."

"People can get run over by a bus," she reminded him. "Or by an avalanche." She decided to seize the moment. "You admit there's an attraction. Why not see where it leads?" she asked boldly, fully expecting him to shoot down the idea. But she could plant the seed, so to speak.

"Are you thinking marriage and babies?"

Her heart set up a clamor. "I'm not seeing quite that far into the future," she said and immediately knew she was lying. She had thought of a future for them, not exactly in concrete terms, but as a possibility. "I've never had an affair. I think it's time."

He muttered a curse. "Are you telling me you've never…that you're a…"

"Virgin? Yes." She met his incredulous glance. "What guy would try anything with a girl who had five older male relatives breathing down his neck? I hardly had a date in high school and college because of them."

"What about now? You're on your own, and your brothers and cousins live in Lost Valley."

"My boss is pretty great. Maybe I'll go for him," she said flippantly.

Adam grabbed her wrist and shook her arm. "Don't do anything stupid. You're not the type for a casual toss in the sack."

"Then what type am I?" she asked rather forlornly.

"Walk," he advised.

She realized they had stopped while they argued their points. They continued their cooldown along the winding trail by the river bank. The rush of the water drowned out other sounds, and it was as if they were alone in the world.

Adam, the first man, she mused. But she wasn't the first woman. She wasn't the Eve he wanted for his paradise.

"So are you looking at Geena as a female friend while you're here on assignment?"

"Perhaps." His smile was somewhat rueful. "She's pretty and smart and accomplished. However, she wants to lead. I'm not a good follower."

"Are you a good lover?"

There was a beat of silence while he frowned, then he ruffled her hair as if she were a youngster. "I do my best," he murmured. "Hey!" he called.

Roni saw Geena on the tennis courts. She waved a racket in their direction. "Anyone for a game?"

"Give me a minute," Adam said and jogged up the terrace steps and into the house.

"Looks as if you had a run," the older woman commented.

Roni nodded. "I try to stick with my program."

Geena wrinkled her nose. "I detest exercise for its own sake. But games are fun. Golf. Tennis. I like playing against a man." Her eyes darted toward the house with a satisfied light in their depths.

Roni wondered if her hostess was thinking of last night and felt sort of sorry for both of them. Geena didn't seem to know she hadn't a chance with the very masculine, very remote male coming toward them, tennis racket in hand.

Apparently no woman did. With that daunting thought, Roni waved absently at the couple and went inside to shower, pack and prepare to leave.

When Scott finally appeared for breakfast, she'd been waiting for over two hours. "Are you ready to head back to town?" she asked, trying to keep the impatience from showing. She had already concluded that a man who was a late riser wasn't for her.

"Not yet." He drank down a glass of orange juice, poured a cup of coffee and placed two muffins on a plate before joining her at the table. "I think we're supposed to be here for cocktails and dinner tonight. Geena invited some people over."

"I hadn't planned on staying that late."

She hushed when Geena and Adam entered, bringing the freshness of the spring morning with them. From their heated bodies came the pleasant scent of perfume and aftershave.

"Do you need to leave?" Adam asked, catching the last part of the conversation.

Roni nodded.

"I'll be heading for town as soon as I shower and change. Do you want a ride?"

"Yes, please."

Scott looked petulant. His sister's face remained pleasant, but the sharp glance she gave Roni was anything but pleased.

"I wish you didn't have to go so early," she murmured to Adam, standing close to him as he drank down a glass of water.

"All good things come to an end." He set the water tumbler on a buffet tray. "Twenty minutes," he said to Roni.

She nodded, refusing to notice the frowns on the other two faces. "It has been fun," she assured Scott, breaking the strained silence.

"Maybe we can do it again. Soon."

His gaze was much too frank as he gave her a hopeful stare. She tried to discourage him without also being rude or harsh. "I'll be starting on a new project tomorrow. That will mean long hours for a few days…maybe weeks."

Adam reappeared on time, suitcase in hand. She dashed up the steps and gathered her case and purse. After bidding the brother and sister goodbye, she and Adam left in his late-model car, which, like hers, had four-wheel drive.

After a couple of miles, she spoke. "Watch yourself. Geena thinks there's something between you."

"I can handle Geena."

"You have lipstick on your mouth."

He wiped it away.

That tiny barb of defeat speared through her again. "I've never felt so odd as I have this weekend," she admitted, worried about the strangeness of it all.

"How's that?"

"As if I've lost something important to me."

He flicked her a glance, then peered back at the road. "You're spoiled. People give you what you want."

"Not you," she said very softly.

He heard, anyway. "I don't have anything for you. Geena knows the score. If I were going to get involved with a woman, she would be my type."

"Ouch." Roni pretended to pull an arrow from her chest.

"Did it pierce your pride?" he asked.

"Yes, and got dangerously close to my heart."

"Ha!" was his response to that.

She forced a laugh. "Well, it could have. Fortunately I keep my heart under lock and key while I wait for someone like my uncle Nick to come along. He's my paradigm of manhood—strong, wise, gentle, loving."

The laughter fled as she realized how much she missed her family. Her brothers had moved their law and medical offices to Lost Valley over the past few months. With their recent marriages, they were busy and preoccupied with establishing their new lives. Only she was left in the city.

As a child, she'd been accidentally left in the woods once. She remembered the darkness, the cold, the terror before the family found her again. Uncle Nick had been furious with the boys, but it had been her fault for following them when she'd been told to stay at the house.

Glancing at her companion, she wondered if the memory held a lesson for her. Adam was a man who preferred to travel alone. A woman would be foolish to chase after him.

Neither of them spoke another word until he dropped her off at her cottage. "Keep looking for that special man," he advised, placing her suitcase on the porch. "Don't settle for less."

Then he left.

Roni had to go to the office on Monday. The design team would be meeting all that week as they planned the next project—a computer game that would appeal to girls.

"Girls are too hard to please," Jerry Bryns, her boss, complained. He looked up from his notes and grinned at her.

He really was heart-stoppingly handsome. Part Latino, he had a brilliant smile and unexpected green eyes with long, black eyelashes. He was also a workaholic who dated the local pool of beautiful women when he had time. Which wasn't often.

"You just have to know what we like," she retorted.

"Which is?" one of the other designer-programmers demanded. He was originally from India and they called him G-2 at his request because his name was too long to pronounce, but had a couple of G's in it.

G-2 had recently married a bride, sight unseen, sent to him by his parents from his home country. He seemed pleased with the arrangement. Roni had thought it odd in this day and age, but sort of romantic, too.

Realizing the men were looking at her, she said, "Well, I like crosswords and jigsaw puzzles. I don't mind fighting off the bad guys to reach a goal, but I like to use my brain, too."

Jerry studied her. "You may not be typical, being raised in a household of guys and all."

"True, but men and women have certain innate characteristics that are stronger in one than the other. I think we need mentors to coax her along." She considered.

"Three of them. Two are on her side, but one is a traitor. Our heroine would have to pick whose advice to follow."

The men liked that idea.

"The good mentors can't always be right and the bad one can't always be wrong, else she'll figure out right away who to believe," Jerry told them.

Roni nodded. "It will have to come down to a battle between our heroine and the bad mentor—"

"Then the final confrontation with the evil scientist—"

"—who has stolen a think tank of child geniuses—"

"—to use for his own purposes of conquering the world—"

The day passed in a blur as they plotted the computer world, their minds tuned to mazes and puzzles, clever traps and concealed escape routes. At five o'clock, Jerry's secretary told them good-night. At nine, her boss rubbed his neck and tossed his pencil aside. "I've had it," he said.

"We have the crux of it," G-2 said in satisfaction.

Roni agreed. She tucked her notes into a folder. "You want to put your stuff in here?"

She stored the ideas in the safe, then closed it and spun the combination lock. A few minutes later she went out into the soft twilight and drove home.

The light blinked on her phone when she got in. She hit the button and listened to the messages.

Roni, this is Patricia. Are you going to be available for lunch on Friday? Let me know.

She wondered why Patricia thought she wouldn't.

Roni, uh, Seth here. Don't forget your birthday dinner at the ranch this weekend. Are you coming up Friday or Saturday? Let Uncle Nick know.

Ah, that was why Patricia had asked about Friday, in case she left town early.

Roni studied the calendar. Actually her birthday was the thirteenth, which was tomorrow, but with the family increasing due to marriages and babies, they had decided to get together on a weekend so they could all be present and celebrate the recent birthdays at once. She and Uncle Nick would share a cake this time.

After thinking it over, she decided she would go up late Friday night, take a long ride on Saturday morning, then help Uncle Nick with the dinner that evening. She made arrangements for lunch with Patricia, then called her relative.

"Where were you?" Uncle Nick asked. "I tried to call three times. You know I hate those machines."

Roni smiled. She was well used to her uncle's ways. "Which is why Seth called to leave the message. You've got to get over this fear of technology, Uncle Nick," she told the old man affectionately.

He snorted, as she'd known he would.

"I had to work. We're planning a new game," she explained. "I'll drive up Friday night, but it may be late when I get there. Let's have the dinner on Saturday."

"Okay, that will work," he said. "Adam can pick you up. Call him to make the arrangements. You got his number?"

"No, but I can drive myself. I'm not sure what time I'll be ready to leave."

"No need. Honey wants to include him in the dinner since Saturday is his birthday. They don't have any other family members close by, you know. I'll tell her to have him call you to set it up."

Roni knew there was no use protesting. To do so would raise questions. Uncle Nick was getting old but he was far from senile. They chatted about the ranch, then said good-bye. She hung up, then stared at the phone, wondering how, short of being hospitalized, she could get out of this.

"At least the traffic is light out this way," Roni said on Friday.

Adam grunted in reply.

He had picked her up at her place at eight o'clock and they were breezing up the highway toward Lost Valley. That would take an hour, barring accidents and traffic jams, then they would have another forty-five minutes to an hour on winding roads before arriving at the ranch tucked into the shadow of the Seven Devils Mountains.

The mountains got their name from an Indian legend about seven devil-monsters who used to raid the villages and eat the children until Coyote got all the sharp-clawed animals to dig really deep holes, which trapped the monsters the next time they appeared. Then Coyote turned them into seven mountain peaks and formed an impassable canyon using the Snake River, so that no more monsters could follow.

"I used to have nightmares about the devils building a bridge to cross Hells Canyon and coming to get us kids," she said, her gaze on the west where the sky glowed in the pink and magenta hues of sunset. "Do you know the story of the original seven devils?"

"Yes."

"I used to know their names. He-Devil. She-Devil. Those are the easy ones." She tried to recall the other peaks that gave the mountains the legend and their name. "The Devil's Tooth. The Ogre."

"Mount Ogre," he corrected. "Mount Baal.

"That's right. And the Goblin is one."

"The Tower of Babel is the seventh."

"Right." She smiled, pleased that they'd gotten all of the names. "Growing up on the ranch, sometimes the peaks seemed as much a part of my family as my brothers and cousins. Did you notice there's only one female peak among the seven?"

He flicked her a glance. "As there was only one female in the Dalton household for most of your life?"

She thought of her aunt Milly and cousin Tink. "Once there were three of us."

Adam nodded when she glanced at him. He wore jeans with boots—real ones, not the fancy kind with high heels and pointed toes—and a chambray shirt with the sleeves rolled up. His hair was freshly trimmed.

"The first time we met, your hair was long and you had a beard and mustache. You looked…forbidding." She laughed. "That's the way you usually look around me."

"The first time we met was at the hospital. Your cousin had been shot while working with me on a case."

"I blamed your sister for bringing evil into our peaceful valley. That was terrible."

He dismissed her regret. "You were upset. Honey understood that."

"She was upset, too. They were in love. I didn't realize that at the time."

"Now they're married and expecting a baby, so don't beat yourself up over the past."

His tone was dry, tinged with its usual sardonic amusement, which sometimes caused her to be angry, sometimes flippant and/or sardonic, too. She watched the sky change to deep shades of purple and blue, a haunting sadness rising from deep inside her.

"I'm not. All's well that ends well, as ol' Will was fond of saying."

"He was a personal friend of yours?" Adam inquired.

"I think my uncle knew him," she replied in the same vein. They laughed together. "How's your case doing, or are you not allowed to talk about it?"

He hesitated, then said, "It's coming along fine. Several interesting offshore bank accounts have been set up that my partner and I are tracking."

"For the fake leasing contracts?"

"What do you know about that?" He spoke sharply, as if interrogating a prisoner.

"Nothing much. I watched a television documentary on the subject a few months ago and that was how some crooks handled phony contracts for nonexistent rental equipment. Also, some companies are doing lease-back agreements with foreign governments."

"Those are legal," he told her.

She snorted. "But are they ethical? It seems to me they're for tax evasion."

"You're sharp," he said wryly. "The IRS should hire you to solve their fraud problems."

"I could work for you," she volunteered.

"No, thanks."

His flat refusal ended that discussion.

Dark had descended by the time they reached the long narrow valley ringed by mountains. A reservoir formed a small lake at the north end of town. Adam turned west just before reaching the lake and they headed out along the winding country road that would take them to the even smaller valley were the Seven Devils Ranch was located.

"Where's your boyfriend?" Adam asked after a long silence. "I thought you'd invite Scott up."

"Why didn't you invite Geena?" Roni challenged.

"I didn't feel up to fighting her off the whole weekend. A guy needs some rest at times, you know?"

"Did you think you wouldn't be able to hold out against her charms?" Roni asked, immediately interested in his reactions to the other woman.

"I don't have that problem where she's concerned."

Her heart bolted. "Only with me?" she asked softly.

From the dim lights on the dash, she saw him frown fiercely. The glance he shot her way wasn't friendly.

"I didn't say that."

"Maybe not, but even I can tell when a man isn't responding. You weren't very happy when she climbed into your lap and wouldn't budge that night in your room."

"Maybe that was because I knew we had an audience."

Roni thought it over and shook her head. "When Scott and I found you in the rose arbor, she was doing all the…the making out. You were enduring."

"The bureau doesn't like their agents to get personally involved while on a case."

His repressive tone told her to drop the subject. She ignored it. "You're involved when we kiss."

"You're an expert, I take it?"

"Yes."

The brakes slammed on. Luckily her seat belt held her securely in place. She gave him a startled glance.

Alone in the middle of the empty road, the twin beams of the headlights were useless against the darkness, which seemed as profound as that of a tomb. The hair rose on the back of her neck, and she felt danger sweep over her like a cold unseen hand.

She shivered.

"Show me," he challenged. "Show me all you know about how I kiss and how involved I am."

"I never back down from a dare," she warned, not sure how they'd gotten to this point, but determined to see it through.

He released his seat belt. "Then show me."

Her breathing deepened and became ragged. She could remember being little and running after her brothers, afraid of being left behind in the woods, afraid of being lost in the mountains where monsters might lurk. She felt the danger of this moment, the darkness all around them…

She spoke calmly. "Remember, you asked for this," she warned, sliding close after releasing her seat belt. "This is how you greeted me that day in the restaurant." She clasped his face between her hands and pressed her mouth to his for a count of five, her eyes open.

So were his.

"There," she said. "That was a friendly kiss. Closed lips, not too much heat. A friend to a friend."

He nodded.

"Then there was the situation in the rose arbor with Geena last weekend. This is the way it might have happened had not Scott and I interrupted."

Roni placed her hands on his shoulders and held him in place so he couldn't move closer, the way he'd been doing with the other woman. She opened her mouth slightly over his, but didn't use any movement or tongue. The embrace lasted maybe ten seconds.

She analyzed the situation when she moved away. "Geena was ardent. You were polite."

"Polite?"

"You didn't want to hurt her feelings with a rejection, so you accepted it when she made the first move and kissed near your mouth. Maybe you turned your head.

At any rate, you weren't involved. She knew that. That's why she was bolder that night in your room."

His smile was skeptical.

Roni gave him a pitying look. "Women know these things," she advised with great assurance. After all, she hadn't observed the males in her family for years without forming some opinions about men and their relationships.

"But you think I was involved when we kissed? Maybe I was thinking of Geena."

She shook her head. "You were involved."

"Show me."

She hesitated.

"Afraid?" he challenged.

"No, I'm not afraid."

His mocking laughter wafted around them. "You should be. I want you…but you know that."

"You would never take an unwilling woman," she said with total conviction.

"Would you be unwilling?"

He moved closer. His warmth surrounded her like a blanket, reaching all the way inside to a place that was suddenly vulnerable and maybe…maybe a little scared, not of him, but of her own feelings.

"No," she whispered, "I wouldn't be unwilling. Not with you."

He closed his eyes as if in pain. "Don't you know better than to say things like that to a man?"

When he glared at her once more, her composure returned. She smiled and shook her head. She wanted to show him just how it could be for them, that what they felt for each other could be real…

She closed her eyes and slowly moved her arms around his shoulders. Slowly, she touched his mouth with hers, but only briefly. She dropped tiny kisses over his lips, from corner to corner, then back to the middle.

With the tip of her tongue, she traced the lines of his mouth, then pushed—ever so slightly—between his lips and explored there. His lips softened, then parted on a sigh.

Tilting her head, she deepened the kiss, exploring the edge of his teeth with her tongue, then playfully coaxing him to join her.

A shudder went through him and echoed in her. She tightened her embrace.

His arms came around her. At the same time, his seat slid back, then he lifted her so that she sat in his lap, their bodies melded together.

"Yes," she whispered. "The kiss deepens because we both want it…because neither of us can help ourselves."

He stopped the words with his lips, taking hers without gentleness, but without harshness, either. His tongue explored her mouth, fought a passionate duel with hers, then licked hungrily over her lips.

The kiss lasted until the sounds of their gasps filled the silence, until she was dizzy from lack of air and knew he was, too. He broke the contact and pressed her head against his shoulder.

"This is madness," he said.

"But sweet." She laved his throat with kisses.

"Your family would hang me if…" He didn't finish the thought.

"My family isn't involved."

She felt his almost silent laugh against her breasts. "With the Daltons, one gets the whole clan."

His words stung. She put her hands on his chest and pushed away a couple of inches. "Well, your sister is already part of us. She looks pretty happy about it."

He placed her in the passenger seat. "You have a great family, Little Bits," he told her, leaning close to give her a serious perusal. "But I'm not the one for you."

She had no answer to that. After tucking her hair behind her ears, she smoothed her summer-weight sweater over her jeans.

"One more thing before we go," he said huskily.

Giving him a puzzled glance, she was startled when he bent close, his head pressing against the underside of her breasts. He eased her sweater out of the way, then kissed her navel, careful of the tiny cross she wore.

"Why did you put an earring here?" he asked, lifting the cross with one finger and studying it.

"Patricia and I decided to do it during our freshman year at college. We went in together and bought the earring set, then had our navels pierced so each of us could wear one. It was a bond between us, our vow to be friends forever."

He sat up and pulled the sweater into place once more. "Yes, that's you," he said, as if that explained all he needed to know about her.

Putting the car in gear, he drove on down the road to the ranch. She saw less than ten minutes had passed since he had slammed on the brakes.

Funny how time seemed to stop when they kissed.

Chapter Five

Honey ran out on the porch when they arrived a few minutes after ten. "I'm so glad you're here. We were getting worried."

Since there weren't a bunch of vehicles in front of the horse rail at the ranch house, Roni wondered who of her family might be there. For the first time that she could recall, she dreaded facing her inquisitive clan.

"I was running late today," she told Adam's sister, who was also Zack's wife and therefore her cousin-in-law.

Honey gave her a hug. "Go on in. Uncle Nick is waiting. Adam, what are you doing? Hurry up, slowpoke."

Inside, Roni dropped her suitcase on the floor and rushed to hug her favorite relative as if she hadn't seen him in months.

Uncle Nick patted her head, then held her off so he

could look her over intently. Smiling, Roni held still for his scrutiny. Growing up, she'd wanted very much to be as old as her brothers and do everything they did, so this was an ancient game between her and her uncle.

"Yes," he finally said, "three gray hairs and as many new wrinkles. You're definitely a year older."

Laughing, they turned to the other two.

"Hey, pug," Adam said, coming in the door and using his pet name for his sister.

Honey hugged him fiercely, then grinned mischievously. "Guess what?" Before he could speak, she added, "You're going to be an uncle."

"An uncle?" he said as if perplexed, then, "You don't mean...are you and Zack...you're expecting?"

"Yes!"

Roni's eyes stung even as she grinned. Honey's joy was contagious, but it also caused a riffle in that river of odd bittersweet sadness that flowed somewhere deep inside her as of late. She was glad Adam hadn't confessed he already knew of his sister's condition.

"So where's the proud father?" Adam demanded.

Honey wrinkled her nose. "He's on duty, but he should be here in an hour or so. Uncle Nick taught me how to make a cherry cobbler today, so we have dessert. Have you two had dinner?"

"Yes, we ate in the city."

"It was my fault we got off so late," Roni admitted, giving the others an apologetic grimace. "We had a meeting at work that took longer than we expected, then

I still had to throw some clothes together while Adam waited patiently."

Honey nodded. "Roni, I put you in the rose room—"

"No, no. That's where you and Zack stay."

"We're using Zack's old room tonight, but we've moved into the house on the property that we bought in town. We're hoping to repair and paint the outside this summer. Adam, you have the room you stayed in last time."

"Where's Trev?" Roni asked.

"Out on the range, repairing fences. He'll be back in time for the birthday dinner."

Roni realized she and Adam would have the west wing to themselves and that only a wall would separate them.

Adam spoke up. "Right. I'll put my things away, then join you for that cobbler. My mouth is already watering."

"Good." Honey headed for the kitchen.

Uncle Nick followed. "Hurry up, you two."

Adam and Roni picked up their luggage. He gestured for her to go first. She was aware of him behind her in the narrow hallway along the west wing.

He went into the next-to-last room while she continued to the very last one, the rose room, they had called it, because of the old-fashioned cabbage rose wallpaper and the roses on the bed coverlet. The room extended the depth of the house and contained a sitting area with a table and reading lamp at one end, the bed at the other, plus a private bathroom next to a large closet. A much-loved baby doll observed her from a pink stroller parked beside a tall willow basket. The basket held a sheaf of dried grasses and long spikes of wild oats.

Roni placed her suitcase in the closet where only extra blankets and pillows were now stored. Once it had been filled with her jeans, shirts, prom dresses and a cheerleader outfit. That seemed a lifetime ago.

Hearing voices from the center of the house, she washed up and joined the others in the kitchen.

"Ice cream?" Honey wanted to know as soon as she entered.

"Please." Roni sat at the kitchen table with Adam while his sister prepared the treat and Uncle Nick poured glasses of milk.

"There's decaf coffee," the older man said. "We can have it and catch the weather on TV when we finish here."

Sitting around the old oak table as she had hundreds of times in the past, the years seemed to fall away. She was eighteen again and living in the bosom of her family, the house and its residents familiar and comforting.

Roni inhaled slowly, carefully, feeling oddly vulnerable at this moment. It was as if she'd been on a long journey the past few years and had thought she might never return.

She shook her head slightly. What was wrong with her equilibrium these days?

Catching Adam's eyes on her, she sought the calm center that existed in every person, according to the book on yoga she'd once read. "It's good to be home again," she said.

Their uncle said good-night after the weather report.

The other three waited for Zack. He arrived a few minutes after eleven o'clock. Honey served him a bowl of cobbler, then they sat in the living room and talked until one-thirty in the morning.

"Alison's baby is the sweetest thing," Honey told Roni after they discussed her due date and whether she and Zack wanted a boy or a girl. "He's smiling now."

"So soon?" Roni asked. "I thought they had to be older to respond."

"He had a gas pain," was Zack's diagnosis.

"Well, Travis, Alison and I think he smiled," Honey declared stoutly while her husband ruffled her hair.

Roni's eyes were drawn to Adam as the couple, sitting together on the leather sofa, teased each other. He glanced at her, then away, his gaze cool and forbidding.

She tried to imagine him as a father, but the image wouldn't quite come. At present, he seemed as distant as He-Devil peak, aloof and above it all.

Adam woke to the first bright rays of sunlight filtering through the lace curtains. He liked the sunrise, always had.

Another day, another chance to excel, his father had been fond of saying.

He didn't know about the excelling part, but for himself, he found his expectations of life brightened with the rising of the sun.

"Ever the optimist," he muttered with more than a little irony as he threw back the cover.

Next door, he heard the shower come on. Roni was up.

His body came to life in the nether regions as he immediately thought of starting the day by showering with her. Other images followed. Talking about babies last night had made him uncomfortable. Each time he'd glanced at Roni, he'd had visions of her slight form rounded with child.

His child.

He cursed under his breath. That would never happen, not in this lifetime. He never planned on having kids.

After pulling on a pair of jeans, he grabbed his toiletry case and headed for the other bathroom on that side of the house. Twenty minutes later, he entered the kitchen.

Uncle Nick—Adam had finally gotten used to calling the older man by the familiar name—was at the table. Roni was breaking eggs into a bowl. They both greeted him.

"Scrambled eggs?" she asked, holding up the bowl.

"Yes, thanks." His heart raced around his chest like a whirling dervish. Like him, she wore jeans and a T-shirt with a long-sleeved shirt over it and open down the front. Like him, she was in her socks, the same as her uncle. Shoes usually came off at the door of the ranch house.

He helped himself to coffee.

"It'll be another hour before the paper gets here," Nick told him. "I checked the TV. Nothing new happening in the world. The weather should be clear for the weekend."

"Good," Adam said.

"Zack and Honey will sleep late," the older man continued. "Roni wants to go for a ride this morning. Are you going?"

Adam nodded. He liked riding in the morning, too. It made him feel like a knight-errant, or something equally romantic, to roam the land as if searching for dragons. He smiled at the ridiculous notion.

Roni gave him a quizzical glance, then lightly buttered several slices of toast. She arranged the eggs, toast and strawberries on three plates and brought them to the table.

"Did you sleep okay?" she asked him.

It was a polite hostess inquiry. He thought of telling her about the images that had first made him restless. "Like a baby," he assured her. Oddly, he did feel rested after the short night. Maybe his dreams had been peaceful.

Thirty minutes later, he rode out on a gelding he particularly liked for its smooth gait. Roni rode a mare who had foaled last fall. The long-legged colt was allowed to run free beside his dam.

He didn't even ask where they were going. It didn't matter. Here on the ranch he was free in a way he'd never felt in the city. He had no duties to perform, no crime to investigate, no deadlines looming.

Roni laughed as the colt nudged her leg with an inquisitive nose, as if asking what she was doing on his mama's back. She scratched his ears, then pushed him away.

Adam's gelding followed the mare along a gravel

road across the ranch pasture. They turned onto a trail after a while. It was cooler in the shade as they made their way through a forest of evergreens. He'd been this way before, so he knew where they were going.

Roni stopped at a tiny creek after an hour's climb and let the horses drink. Neither of them spoke as they wound their way higher up the mountain. At last they came out on a granite ledge.

"The Devil's Dining Room," she called out, glancing over her shoulder at him.

He nodded. A huge, flat-topped boulder gave the place its name. One end of it jutted out over the cliff. A smaller boulder formed a stool, the Devil's Seat, one of the Daltons had explained on a previous visit.

They dismounted, leaving the horses ground-hitched. Which meant lifting the reins over the gelding's head and letting them trail on the ground. The animals were trained to stay in the area but were free to munch on the spring grass.

So far this maneuver had worked, but he'd always had his doubts about it. At least it was downhill, in case they had to walk back to the house.

Roni climbed on the stool, then hoisted herself onto the big boulder. She sat on the edge sticking out into thin air and dangled her feet over. It looked like a thousand feet down to him. She patted the space next to her.

"Are you sure that will hold two people?" he asked.

"We always sit here."

"You Daltons lead charmed lives," he grumbled, but he climbed up and took his place.

"I love it here," she told him. She breathed deeply and let it out in an audible sigh of contentment.

From this vantage point, he could see the homestead tucked into its narrow valley. Tulips and daffodils bloomed along the paddock fence and the sides of the house while rose bushes held pride of place in the front yard.

"Look," she said, pointing, "you can see Travis and Alison's house through the trees."

He spotted the roof of the couple's home. Smoke drifted lazily on the morning breeze. "Looks as if they have a fire going."

"Alison loves a fire, so Travis builds one to take the chill off on cool mornings."

"The things a man will do for a woman," he said with cynical amusement.

"He loves her. People in love do thoughtful things for each other."

Adam frowned at the earnest tone as Roni explained love and marriage to him. She needed to curb her idealistic fantasies. It could get her hurt someday.

"He does it for the sex."

Instead of getting angry, she laughed. "Well, there is that." Giving him an oblique perusal, she added, "It's what keeps civilization going."

He observed the curve of her lips, the confidence in her eyes, the challenge in the tilt of her chin. He leaned closer. "I'm willing to do my part," he said in his most cynical manner.

She didn't retreat. Meeting him halfway, she stroked his cheek. "Would you give me a child, Adam?"

Was it imagination or did the boulder tremble? He moved away from her playful touch and gazed a thousand feet down the cliff, acutely aware that they were on a precipice and that it wasn't because of the mountain ledge.

"No." he said flatly.

"I want a family," she said in a soft, dreamy way. "Two children would be perfect. Or three or four."

Her laughter was the sound of angels singing at twilight, of bells tinkling from far away, of all the longings he'd ever experienced in a lifetime of yearning.

He clasped the edge of the cold, rough granite and fought emotions that he didn't understand, that made him angry and unsure of his chosen path in life.

"I always travel alone," he said in desperation.

"Honey warned me of that."

He snorted. "You women put too much emphasis on relationships and commitment."

She leaned against his arm and rubbed her cheek on his shoulder. "Humans are social animals. We need each other."

The warm scent of her hair wafted over him. He inhaled deeply, then without meaning to, kissed the top of her head.

"That was nice," she murmured, gazing into his eyes.

Her eyes were evenly blue, in the ridges and in the valleys between, enticing him into the magic world of her embrace. He knew he shouldn't enter.

But that didn't stop him from thinking about it and the pleasure he'd find with her.

"Do it," she said.

"What?"

"What your eyes are saying you want. I want it, too."

"Brazen hussy," he chided. It sounded like a caress.

When she grinned, he couldn't keep the smile from his face. She drove him mad with her opinionated ways, frustrated the hell out of him at times and yet…and yet she intrigued him and lured him into the web of her loveliness, her passionate nature and her openly curious interest in making love with him.

"Your family would shoot me for what I'm thinking," he admitted, his voice hoarse with hunger.

"Tell me," she at once urged, her eyelashes dropping to a sexy level.

He wrapped an arm around her and tucked her against his side. With her head on his shoulder, he kissed her lightly several times, then with ever deeper need. The world became smaller until there was only them and the heat from the union of their mouths.

When he shifted uncomfortably, she stroked her hand down his chest. Before he realized what she intended, his jeans were unsnapped and the zipper was sliding down.

"Don't," he gasped, but it was too late.

When she eased the constriction of his briefs, his

arousal surged upright. A hot glow sizzled in his brain. He couldn't think, couldn't speak as she closed her hand very gently and just as gently squeezed.

"You're playing with fire," he warned. "Someone always gets burned."

Roni marveled at the hardness, although she'd expected it. She wasn't naive where men were concerned, only inexperienced. She kissed his throat as little bolts of electricity ran over her nerves.

"I'm burning now," she told him.

"So am I."

"Hold me." It was a plea as the world danced in flames all around her.

He lifted her so that she straddled him, then kissed her in a way that was different from any she'd ever known. She felt him shudder, then wrapping her in a tight embrace, he began to move.

The hard ridge stroked against her, causing her to gasp as pleasure shot deep into her. She instinctively followed his lead, pressing into that tempting hardness, feeling sensation flow between them like arcs of molten gold at every pressure point—their lips, their chests, their thighs.

Just when she thought she would burst from so much wild hunger, he groaned, jerked his lips from hers and set her away from him. Pushing to his feet, he turned his back.

"We must be insane," he said, adjusting his clothing.

Her trembling legs would hardly support her as she stood.

He wiped sweat from his brow with a sleeve, then lightly leaped to the shorter boulder and onto the ground. "Come on, Little Bits. We need to be around people."

She followed him silently to their mounts. Heading down the trail, she wasn't sure what she regretted more—stopping or not finishing what they had started.

Roni rose from the bed and slipped on her boots. She may as well get up since she couldn't sleep. After lunch, she'd determinedly gone to her room to rest. But now, hearing her twin cousins—Trevor and Travis—in the paddock, she went outside to see what was going on.

"Hey, Roni," Trevor called. "We could use a hand here."

She climbed up on the top rail. "What's happening?"

Travis removed his hat and swiped a bandanna over his face. "New horse," he said, nodding toward a cream-colored gelding with black mane and tail.

"He's a beauty," she said. "What's his problem?"

Trevor stood in the middle of the paddock, reins in hand. "Dropsy. He should have been put down when he was a yearling. The owner is a fifteen-year-old girl and her parents want us to get the horse in shape."

She grimaced in sympathy. Some horses were born with a fear of the world, it seemed. Every new thing, or even an old one at times, would frighten them so much, they would go down in a dead faint.

"He takes the saddle okay," she said.

"That much progress has taken a month," Travis said

with a disgust that was surprising for him. He was usually the quieter and more patient of the twins.

Trevor looked her over, then said to his brother, "Roni doesn't weigh more than a hundred pounds. Think she could ride him?"

Roni looked at Travis.

"Would you be willing to try?" he asked. "I think he was treated harshly by a previous owner and is scared of men."

"Sure," she said. "You think he's ready?"

"Atta girl," Trevor approved. "Trav, help me box him in against the fence, then Roni can get on."

He led the suspicious horse to the corner where the fence joined the stable. When he and Travis were in position, Roni crossed the paddock.

"What's his name?"

"Ranger."

As she neared the nervous horse, she began speaking in a low croon. "Hey, Ranger. Good boy. There, now, nothing bad is going to happen. Good boy. Easy, now. Easy."

She stroked his neck as he rolled his eyes. She let him sniff her hand, then she stroked and talked some more.

"Ready when you are," she finally told her cousins.

"Okay," they said in unison.

She put her foot in the stirrup and gave a little jump so that she could reach the saddle horn. The muscles under the gelding's skin rippled uncontrollably.

"Easy, Ranger. It's okay. We're going for a ride. You'll like that."

Travis had both hands against the horse's left flank. He moved one so that Roni could swing into the saddle. As soon as she was mounted, she felt the horse tremble under her...not unlike the way Adam had trembled against her that morning, she reflected. A flush of heat settled in her tummy at the memory.

Trevor cursed. "Hold on, he's going down. You got the switch?"

Travis pulled a switch from his boot and used it on the horse's backside in hopes that Ranger would be more afraid of the switch than the weight on his back.

Roni kept up a steady stream of chatter. Trevor pulled on the reins, forcing the head up. Each time the back legs buckled, Travis used the switch to keep the animal on its feet. At last the fainting spell passed.

"Damn stupid horse," Trevor muttered, but softly. "Ready?"

"Yes," she said.

Travis stood aside while Trevor walked the gelding around the paddock three times. "Think you can take him now?" Trev asked.

She nodded. "He feels fine to me."

Guiding the horse around the paddock, she prodded him into a trot after several rounds, then a canter. "Great gait," she said, passing the twins, who had moved slowly to the stable door while she worked the mount.

At that moment, several things happened. A parcel post truck arrived. The driver tooted the horn to let Uncle Nick know he had a delivery. At the same moment, Adam came around the corner of the barn and climbed up on the fence to get a better view of what was going on.

Roni felt the knotting of every muscle in her mount as the gelding went into a spasm of fear. She automatically stood in the stirrups as she felt the animal rear up. At the height of the lift, she felt the sudden and absolute release of those muscles. Several hundred pounds of horse flesh went toppling over backwards.

"Jump!" she vaguely heard male voices shouting.

What the heck did they think she was trying to do? she wondered in vexation. Using her knees to take the weight off her feet, she kicked one foot free. The other was stuck between the horse and the fence.

She threw herself at the fence as Ranger collapsed, felt a wrench when her right foot caught, scrabbled like mad to hold onto a rail, lost it and banged her head on three other rails on the way down. Her foot slipped free and she felt her back on the ground.

Thrusting as hard as she could, she shoved the gelding one way, herself another. Her momentum took her under the bottom rail and she rolled safely out of harm's way.

Ranger hit the dirt where she'd been lying a split second ago.

"Don't move her," a very forceful male voice ordered.

Roni opened her eyes. "I know that tone," she said, struggling to sit up.

"Be still," Adam said in a snarl.

He and the other two men crouched around her, their faces drawn with worry.

"I'm fine," she said. "Really."

"If anyone has a gun handy, I'm going to shoot that horse," Trevor declared.

Roni let Adam help her to her feet, his arms supporting most of her weight as she stood and took inventory. Nothing was broken that she could tell. She put a hand to her head.

"I think I'm going to have a doozy of a headache in the near future," she said.

Adam swept her into his arms. "You need to rest."

She snuggled against him, loving the fresh-laundry smell of his shirt, the scent of his aftershave and the hot, sweaty aroma of his body that told her how much he'd feared for her.

"I love a strong, masterful man," she said, then wondered where she'd heard those words recently before the world went hazy, then vague…very, very vague.

Chapter Six

"I'm fine," Roni repeated for what seemed like the hundredth time. She smiled at her older brother, Seth, and Amelia, his wife, who owned a local bed and breakfast inn.

Seth and Amelia had known each other forever, but finally last year friendship had blossomed into love and they had married. The family had also learned that Seth wasn't a half brother to her and Beau as they had thought. However, he had been part of the Daltons since his mother had died in the avalanche that killed her father, so Roni still thought of Seth as a brother.

The family had gathered tonight for the joint birthday dinner celebrating her twenty-seventh birthday, Adam's thirty-seventh one and Uncle Nick's seventy-first.

Roni rarely thought of her uncle as old—he was as enduring as He-Devil peak—so she was surprised each year at his age. However, his mortality had been brought home to her last year when he'd had a heart attack. He'd had a couple of spells since then, too.

A slight depression settled over her even as she smiled and chatted with her brothers, cousins and the four women who were now part of the Dalton gang.

"Are you okay?" Adam asked, as if sensing her downturn in spirits. He sat on an ottoman next to her.

"I'm fine," she said yet again.

She held pride of place in the big leather easy chair due to her fall and hadn't been allowed to help with dinner preparations. However, she had held her nephew— Logan Nicholas Dalton, born March third—until he'd fallen asleep on her shoulder. He was now in the refurbished nursery next to Uncle Nick's room.

"Okay, everyone, quiet," Zack called from the kitchen. "Seth, turn out the lights."

In the dark, they waited. From the kitchen came a muffled curse. That brought forth chuckles from the living room. Finally, Zack, Honey and Alison came in, each carrying a birthday cake ablaze with candles. As if on cue, the whole bunch started singing, "Happy birthday."

Zack stopped in front of the family patriarch, Honey in front of Adam and Alison in front of her.

"Blow," Zack ordered at the end of the song.

Roni blew as hard as she could. Adam finished his,

then leaned close and gave her a little help. The scent of his aftershave and shampoo was familiar, exciting and oddly comforting. Looking at the new family brides, she wondered if she would ever be one of them.

When all the candles were extinguished, Seth switched the lights on. Three presents, which had been hidden behind the sofa, were handed out. All three were white cowboy hats for summer. Wearing their new finery, the birthday honorees cut their cakes. Alison and Honey then distributed the slices on festive paper plates with matching forks and napkins.

After the treat, they talked about the opening of the resort. They had finally settled on Lost Valley Lodge for a name. The grand opening was planned for the end of the month. Hiring was in progress with Seth, the attorney, and Zack, the deputy, in charge of interviews and background checks. Since the men knew nearly everyone in the area, Roni thought that wouldn't take long.

"Ah, life is good," her brother Beau said. He and Shelby and their son, Nicky, sat on the floor between the sofa and the other easy chair where Uncle Nick sat.

Honey, Seth and Amelia were on the leather couch while Zack also sat on the floor and leaned against Honey's knees. Trevor, the last bachelor in the clan, was in the kitchen helping himself to another sample from the three cakes—one chocolate, one coconut and hers, a heavenly concoction of yellow cake with a can of drained mandarin oranges whipped into the batter, then frosted with whipped cream containing pineapple bits and vanilla instant pudding. Her aunt Millie had called it a Hawaiian wedding cake.

At ten o'clock Uncle Nick rose and announced he was going to bed. The others dispersed, too, leaving her and Adam and Trevor.

"I think I'll turn in, too," Trev decided. "Roni, you're sure you're okay?"

"I'm sure." She smiled brightly to convince him.

Since she'd slept most of the afternoon, she stayed with Adam to catch the news and weather on TV. After that, she went to her room and changed from slacks and a plaid shirt into a nightshirt that buttoned down the front.

A good thing, she decided, wincing as she moved her shoulder. She didn't think she could lift her right arm above chin height. There was also a nice lump on the back of her head.

Still not sleepy after brushing her teeth and washing her face, she decided to read a chapter in the novel she'd brought with her. She loved the story of the young wizard and his trials and tribulations. Her world was downright tame compared to his. After reading the chapter, she decided to indulge in one more. After all, she could sleep late.

Adam's voice startled her. "Roni?"

"Yes?" she called softly.

He opened the door, spotted her in the chair, then entered and closed the door silently. He held up a yellow tube of ointment. "I have something for that shoulder—an analgesic cream. That should help the soreness."

She was grateful for the kindness. "I didn't realize I'd hit so many places." She felt the goose egg on the back of her head.

"You should have kept the ice on that," he advised, "and the shoulder."

Nodding, she held out her hand, aware that it was late and the bed was only steps away. She glanced down. The nightshirt came past her knees, so that was okay. Her house slippers, warm and fuzzy inside, soft cotton outside, covered her ankles. Nothing that could be construed as provocative was showing.

"I'll rub it in," he volunteered. "Can you pull your top down a bit?"

After checking, she shook her head.

"Unbutton a couple of notches."

She hesitated. The house had been silent for a long time. She'd assumed Adam and the others were snug in their beds. "Why aren't you asleep?" she asked.

"I saw the light under your door when I went to my room. Earlier I saw you grimace when you handed the baby to Alison. It looked as if you were in pain."

Nodding, she flicked open the top two buttons and partially turning her back to him, slipped the nightshirt off her sore shoulder.

He knelt on one knee and muttered an imprecation. "You're bruised all the way across your shoulder. Why didn't you say something? Beau could have checked it out while he was here. Maybe you should have an X ray."

"Nothing's broken, so there's no need to cause a fuss. I've taken worse falls than that one."

"Yeah? How many times has a ton of horse flesh fallen on you?" he demanded.

"He didn't weigh a ton, only about fifteen hundred pounds, I should think." She tossed him an insouciant grin over the bare shoulder, then batted her eyelashes sexily.

He snorted, then sighed. "It's your upbringing, I suppose. You just have to keep up with the men in your family. Honey and Amelia think you were afraid of being left behind while growing up. Because of losing your parents."

"You lost your parents, too," she softly reminded him.

Refusing to acknowledge that bond between them, Adam screwed open the medicine tube, laid the top on the table where she'd placed the book, then squirted a generous dollop onto his palm. He spread it over her shoulder.

Inhaling sharply, he admitted he'd known what her skin would feel like and had anticipated the smoothness of it, the warmth, the way it yielded to his touch. Yet there was solid bone and muscle under it. She was toned and fit.

A tough, fearless and independent tomboy. A loving, loyal sister, niece and cousin. A sexy, lovely woman...

Something shifted painfully inside him as unbidden tenderness washed over him.

He swallowed hard, realizing that while he'd prepared himself for touching her when he came in, he had no defenses where she was concerned. He'd thought he could handle this Good Samaritan effort without a lot of reaction. Ha.

His hand slowed. Gritting his teeth, he added more cream and stroked her neck after pushing her hair aside. He broadened his efforts to include both shoulders as he spotted a tiny bruise on the other side.

"Can you get your arm out?" he asked, unable to disguise the huskiness of desire.

She unfastened another button and slipped the nightshirt down her arm. Then she bared the other arm and tucked the shirt securely under her armpits.

He could see a bit of delectable swell on the right side, just enough to remind him of the shape and feel of her small, perfect breast against his hand. His blood seemed to thicken, making his heart pound with a heavy beat to force it through his body.

Wrenching his thoughts from the feast before him, he spread more of the analgesic across her back, over both shoulders and down her arms, then back to her neck.

She helped by holding her nightshirt with one hand and sweeping her hair on top of her head with her left hand.

"Good," he murmured, his voice a thread of sound in the almost silent room. Only the quick inhalations of their breaths disturbed the quiet.

As gently as possible, he rubbed the medicine into the bruises and bare flesh, adding a bit of pressure down her spine to relax the tight muscles there.

"That's fine," she said. Her voice caught. "You can quit now."

"I don't want to," he admitted, more to himself than to her. He clung to the ragged edge of sanity, but like a fraying rope, sense and reasoning at last snapped. He bent and kissed the vulnerable spot behind her ear.

She gave a little gasp and sat totally still, a tiny wild creature trying to escape detection.

But it was too late. He was aware of her in every cell of his body, in every nook and cranny of his consciousness, in the deepest, darkest secret places where dreams were born…where hope lingered…

She released her hair, and it tumbled over his hand like black silk, a mass of inky waves. He brought a curl to his lips and pressed a kiss in the shining strands. Catching the fresh, lemony scent of it, he inhaled slowly, savoring the clean smell as if it was the rarest of perfumes.

He dropped the curl and put the cap on the medicine tube, then laid it on the table beside her book. He saw the title of the novel and smiled. "You would have fit into that adventure without a wrinkle."

"I always thought flying around on a broomstick sounded like the epitome of fun."

"You *would*," he said with a certain wry amusement.

Her laughter flowed into him, all the way to his soul. His feeble conscience ordered him to get out of her bedroom, to leave and not look back.

He knew it wouldn't happen. Unless *she* told him to go, he couldn't move…

Roni turned her head as if in slow motion. Something had happened during the past minute or so. Something had changed—an element of the universe had shifted and a cosmic force had entered the room and shattered the careful calm of the evening.

Adam was staring at her, his eyes as dark as the night sky. A strand of sun-lightened hair, shining like antique gold in the lamplight, fell over his forehead. He rose from the kneeling position and stepped back one pace.

She, too, pushed to her feet, unsure what was to come but not afraid to face it. Losing her grip on the night-shirt, she felt its downward slide, then it pooled around her hips. She had only to move slightly and…

Adam let his gaze feast upon her for a moment, then he reached out and brushed a finger over the dark pink tips that sat like small jewels on her breasts.

She gave a little gasp.

He had to open his mouth to breathe, too. The air in the room was suddenly too thick. Trailing his finger down her torso, he reached the cotton clinging to her hips. One touch and it fell to the floor.

Her skin glowed in the lamplight like the rarest alabaster. Unlike stone, it was warm and supple when he rested his hand against her. He touched the tiny triangle of curls between her legs.

"Take me," she whispered. "Take me to bed."

He lifted her, this perfect little goddess, and did as she requested.

Roni could have wept at the gentleness of his touch,

the careful way he placed her on the bed and covered her with the sheet. She pushed both pillows behind her back, sure he would leave now, willing herself to accept his rejection yet again.

But no, he wasn't leaving. Without taking his eyes off her, he shucked his jeans and shirt, tossed his socks aside. He wore white briefs. When she held her arms out, he sat beside her and gathered her close.

"What are we doing?" he asked, pressing kisses on her temple. He lay beside her.

"Shh," she said, afraid to break the spell. "Shh."

After several kisses, all carefully controlled on Adam's part, Roni knew he was withdrawing. His indomitable will had conquered the fiery desire.

It was for the best, she acknowledged, although not without a pang of regret. Fatigue washed over her like a spring rain. She yawned, rolled over on her left side and scooted back until she nestled snugly against him.

"Turn out the light," she requested.

She felt his hesitation and knew he warred with his conscience. The battle was his, so she remained quiet and still. At last he flicked off the lamp, then lifted the sheet and curled against her, his knees tucked into the curve of hers, his arm resting across her hip, his head sharing her pillow.

"Nothing is going to happen," he told her.

"Except sleep," she added on a lighter note, seeing the humor in their dilemma of desire and denial.

He sighed heavily, then chuckled. "Except sleep."

* * *

The sky wasn't yet light when a crack of thunder rolled down the valley from the high peaks to the west. Roni woke and listened. She realized Adam was awake, too.

"A storm on the mountain," she murmured.

They lay side by side, her leg casually thrown over his as if they'd slept this way many times. She felt the stir of his body against her hip. His hand slid across her belly as he moved closer. He kissed her bare shoulder.

"I don't want to move," she said on a half groan.

His logic was simple. "Then don't."

"I've got to go to the bathroom."

She felt the low rumble of his laughter against her back. "One, two, three," he intoned.

They rose together, but he went to the window and pulled the curtain aside enough to check the weather while she went into the adjoining bathroom. She brushed her teeth, washed her face and combed her hair before returning.

He went in when she came out.

A shiver ran over her as she climbed into bed. Looking at the clock, she noticed it wasn't yet five o'clock. She pulled the cover up, tucking it under her arms as she rested against the headboard. Then she waited.

Her heart changed its beat when Adam emerged. His masculine form was barely discernible, except for the white band of his briefs. He stopped beside the bed.

Neither spoke as the seconds passed. Neither moved.

At last she couldn't bear the tension. She reached out and stroked the lean, hard muscles of his thigh.

He muttered a harsh word, then caught her hand and held it still against him. The tension mounted until it crackled like a high-voltage charge. When he joined her once more, she sighed in relief.

"Mmm, you're cold," she said, pressing against him.

Gently easing her onto her back, he lay on his side, one leg over hers. Propped on one arm, he placed a hand in the center of her body, examined the navel ring and tickled her belly button before moving upward.

He captured her breast in his hand. She felt her nipple bead against his palm. He brushed lightly back and forth.

Moving one leg so their thighs were sandwiched together, she felt a sharp thrill at the hardness that pressed against her abdomen. She experimented with the various sensations caused by rubbing her thigh over his and then by pressing against that hardness.

A tiny moan escaped her as she tried to push up on her sore shoulder.

He turned them so she lay atop his lithe, masculine form. "Be still," he warned, but with humor. "Go back to sleep."

She smiled and shook her head. Finding she had more range of movement, she was quick to take advantage of it. He moved his hands to her hips and guided her as she stroked against him.

"Take these off," she whispered, tugging at the waistband of his briefs. "I want to feel you against me."

He inhaled sharply, then nodded.

As soon as he had tossed the obstruction to the floor, she straddled his hips, knees supporting most of her weight, and fitted herself against him. "Wonderful," she said as she experimented with the new sensation this produced.

She had only to slide against him the tiniest bit for waves of feeling to rush from that point to all parts of her body. When he cupped both hands over her breasts and caressed the sensitive tips, she closed her eyes and simply enjoyed his touch.

Soon that wasn't enough. She again stretched out on him, her legs on either side of his. He pushed a hand into her hair and held her in place for a deep, long kiss.

They shared a thousand kisses, lips on lips, on throats and breasts. Once he kissed and explored her navel with his tongue, careful of the tiny ring there. Then he urged her to move against him once more.

She was surprised and perhaps a little embarrassed by the moist heat that flowed from her body. Like his arousal, it showed how ready she was for his complete caress.

"Come to me," she whispered, kissing his neck and nipping at his collarbone.

"No, baby. I don't have anything to protect you."

With anyone else, she would have objected to being called "baby," but with this man, she recognized it as an endearment. She didn't think he realized he'd used it.

"It should be okay. It's time for…"

She found she wasn't as candid or as bold with him as she'd pretended. She tried to think of a genteel word.

"Your phase of the moon?" he suggested with a hint of laughter in his deepened voice. "You shouldn't have told me that. It weakens my defenses."

She sighed. "You know I want you so much I ache."

"Yeah, I know the feeling."

He wrapped his arms around her and turned so she was on her back and he was on top. She caught his head between her hands and pulled his mouth to hers. With his weight resting on his elbows to each side of her and his thighs encasing hers, she discovered a new aspect to lovemaking.

"A perfect love nest," she told him, stroking along his sides and over his buttocks, feeling surrounded by his strong, protective presence.

"Open a little," he murmured.

She opened her legs at the pressure, then gasped as she felt him slide between them. His thighs pressed hers closed and he began to move as she'd done to him earlier. Fiery need erupted deep inside her.

"Come to me," she invited once again.

"No," he said and kissed any other words from her lips.

More by accident than design, she found when she curved her hips upward to meet his gentle thrust, the intimacy increased a thousandfold. A movement from either of them would merge them into one.

He immediately stopped. Their eyes locked.

Aeons rushed by, and time became a wind that roared past her ears, blocking all other sounds.

She felt his arms tremble, then he moved his legs between hers and slowly, slowly let his weight sink into her, little by little. She wriggled a bit to accommodate this journey into the greatest intimacy she'd ever experienced.

"Adam," she whispered. "This is…it's…so perfect."

"Am I hurting you?"

He was so sincere, so careful with her, she could have wept. "Not at all."

Then he kissed her a thousand times and slid one hand between them, helping her find the ecstasy his touch had always promised. She clung to him desperately as her body convulsed in pleasure so intense she couldn't breathe.

For a long time, she simply floated in a sea of contentment such as she'd never known.

"I wish I could tell you how marvelous that was," she at last murmured. They lay side by side, still joined in the magic of passion.

He traced the line of her eyebrow and along her cheek to the corner of her mouth with his fingertips. His touch was magic. She moved slightly, experimentally, knowing he hadn't taken his satisfaction.

Somewhat shockingly, she found she wanted him again.

"Once more?" he asked, rolling over her when she nodded and tried not to blush like a schoolgirl.

Gazing up at him, her heart gave a giant leap. Did he

realize the depth of emotion exposed in his eyes? She thought not.

To her delight, he began the rhythmic seduction all over again. She writhed against him, disrupting the rhythm he'd established as hunger flowed through her in increasing surges, like storm waves pounding a shore.

"It's okay," he told her, husky pleasure in the words as he brought them back in sync. "Take what you want."

"You," she whispered, frantic now as the moment drew near. "I want you."

Again she was lost to reality as sensation exploded deep within her and lodged in the most intimate places they touched. She gave a panting moan. He kissed it away.

When she felt him tense, when every muscle in his lithe body went rock hard, she crooned unintelligible sounds of satisfaction and urged him to move in her.

"Don't, baby," he warned.

The muscles flexed in his arms, then he pulled away from her. Using the cotton briefs as a shield between them, he buried his face against her neck and held her tightly.

Against her abdomen, she felt the throbbing beat of his body and heard his heavy sigh as he relaxed. His weight bore down on her, but she didn't mind. She kissed his shoulder and his cheek, then simply wrapped her arms around him and squeezed him as hard as she could in a sudden delirium of happiness.

When he rolled to her left side, ever careful of the sore right shoulder, she snuggled against him in perfect contentment. "That was wonderful," she murmured, then yawned as warmth and languor swept over her in a soothing mist.

"The best," he agreed, running his fingers through her hair.

Curious, she asked, "Why did you move away?"

He curved one thigh over hers and tucked her to him. "A slight precaution. You could get pregnant, anyway, but…"

She felt his shrug that indicated he'd done all he could at the moment. Her last thought before she drifted into enchanting dreams was that she'd like a baby.

His baby, she corrected.

She didn't wake until she heard the sound of her uncle's voice, calling her name.

Chapter Seven

"Roni?"

Roni opened her eyes, confused for only a split second, then she realized where she was...and who was there with her. She turned to Adam, her eyes wide with alarm.

"Roni, are you all right?" Uncle Nick asked, an ominous quietness in his tone that she had rarely heard.

"Uh, yes," she called. She checked the clock. Almost nine. She silently groaned. Until her uncle left that part of the house, Adam was trapped in her room. "I'm fine," she said more strongly.

There was silence on the other side of the door. She strained to hear the sound of retreating footsteps.

"He knows," Adam murmured.

She shook her head.

"Adam seems to be missing," Uncle Nick continued

after a lengthy pause. "His bed doesn't appear to have been slept in. Honey is worried. She wants the boys to go out looking for him." Another pause. "In case he's lost on the ranch."

Adam's chest rose and fell in a resigned breath. "I'm okay," he called. "There's no need for a search."

Another one of those ominous silences, then, "I'll see you in my office in ten minutes," the family patriarch stated in no-nonsense terms. His departure down the hall was loud and clear.

Roni thought she was going to faint as guilt, horror and a host of other emotions descended on her.

"Time to face the music." Adam gave her a brief smile and patted her shoulder. "It'll be okay."

She shook her head in despair at disappointing her beloved relative. "Uncle Nick is old-fashioned. He thinks sleeping together means…" She couldn't continue.

"He advised Honey and Amelia to seduce his nephews, probably Alison and Shelby, too. We can say we were practicing what he's preached for years."

"That was because he knew they would marry." She scrambled from the covers. "We have to dress. We only have ten minutes."

Adam tucked the sheet around her. "He wants to see me, not you. Let me talk to him first."

While Adam pulled on his clothes, she sat like the proverbial pillar of salt, not one iota of an idea in her head to explain this indiscretion.

Observing his calm silence, she couldn't bring herself to regret the night in his arms. Adam had been everything she could have wished for in a lover. She wouldn't let her family insult or abuse him for something she'd wanted and had fully participated in.

"I'm not sorry," she announced and heard the stubborn streak creep into the words.

Adam stopped at the door. For a second there was something like admiration and tenderness in his gaze, then, "Good," he said softly, albeit a trifle grimly. He left the room, closing the door securely behind him.

Roni dashed for the shower. She washed and dressed in record time, moaning once when she lifted her arm to brush her hair and fix it into a ponytail. In blue slacks and a white knit shirt, still wearing her house slippers, she hurried to the ranch office.

When she tried to door, she found it locked. "It's Roni," she called out.

"Wait in the kitchen," Uncle Nick told her. "We'll be out soon. Adam needs some breakfast."

That, she ascertained, meant she was to go and cook it like a good little girl. "I have a right to know what's going on." She rattled the doorknob.

"Everything's fine," Adam assured her. "We'll be out in a minute."

Frustrated and resentful at being excluded, not to mention the guilt at leaving Adam alone with her uncle's wrath, or worst—his expectations for their future, Roni went to the kitchen.

A platter of bacon was on the stove. She stirred up

pancake batter and heated the griddle. Just as she finished taking up the last golden circle, the two men appeared.

She looked from one to the other. Neither looked angry. However, they both studied her with solemn expressions, like doctors wondering how to tell a patient there was no hope. Undefined emotions fluttered through her.

"What?" she said.

"We're engaged," Adam informed her. "We'll head for Nevada after we eat and get married there."

Uncle Nick nodded. He didn't look disappointed in her nor angry at her behavior. In fact, he seemed quite satisfied, the way he'd been after each of the marriage announcements of the preceding year.

She laid the spatula aside and carried the platter of bacon and pancakes to the table. "I'm not going to Nevada."

"Yes, we are," Adam declared.

She shook her head.

Uncle Nick came a step closer and peered into her eyes. "This isn't what you want?" Now he looked a tad uncertain.

"I—I always thought I'd be married at the church in town, that you would give me away. I want to wear Grandma Dalton's wedding dress. It fits me."

She stopped and licked her lips. Voicing the dreams she'd held close to her heart seemed childish in light of the men's practical plans. However, this wasn't exactly her vision of a rapturous engagement.

Didn't dreams count for anything? And what of love?

The two men glanced at each other, shared an unspoken agreement, then Uncle Nick nodded. "Next weekend, then. You two can get your license and all that during the week. The ceremony can be Saturday afternoon at the church."

Roni, feeling as if the air had turned to thick, white syrup, could barely shake her head.

"Let me talk to her," Adam said. "Alone." Taking her arm, he led her to the office and closed the door. "What's the problem, Little Bits?" he asked.

She answered with her own question. "A forced marriage, Adam? That's ridiculous in this day and age."

He studied her for a long minute, his eyes roaming over her as if he could see right through her skin. "There could be a child. I don't want any questions about its birth or its parentage."

She mulled his answer over before asking, "If there is, what happens with the marriage?"

"We make it work." He rubbed a hand over his brow as if a headache was starting. "Honey was three years old when our mom died. I remember how scared she was—"

He stopped as if the memory was too painful to recall. In that instant, Roni realized that Adam's sense of honor, his commitment to responsibility, was as great as her beloved uncle's. Just as Nicholas Dalton couldn't turn his back on six orphans, Adam wouldn't turn from what he saw as his duty, even if it involved marriage.

"I would never run out on a child," he ended.

"And if there isn't one?"

The silence stretched into an aeon. "Let's take it one problem at a time," he finally said. "Who knows? Maybe we'll live happily ever after as you're so fond of predicting."

This was said with an undercurrent of bitterness, as if he didn't think that rosy outlook could ever be true for him. She ached for him, for this boy who'd learned never to hope for too much or trust his happiness to another.

She thought of the intimacy of the night, the wonder of it, the bliss they'd shared. Afterward there had been deep contentment. He'd felt it, too, or he wouldn't have stayed.

Perhaps marriage was the right thing for them. Maybe, just maybe, it was meant to be. Her heart leaped to her throat at the thought. Happily ever after?

"Yes," she murmured, "there is that possibility."

Gazing into his eyes, she knew it would be okay. Adam was an honorable man. He wouldn't leave her behind in the dark forest of regret and unhappiness...

She broke the odd thought and smiled. "Okay," she said, keeping her tone light, "let's give it a fighting chance."

Adam chucked her under the chin. "Atta girl."

"Shall we kiss to seal the bargain?" Her glance from under her lashes was deliberately bold.

His chuckle preceded a gentle kiss. "Now we'd better get back to your uncle."

Arm in arm, they returned to the kitchen. Uncle Nick

looked them over. "Well, then, it's settled. Actually this is perfect. The grand opening of the lodge is Saturday. We can hold the reception there."

The stern visage disappeared, and he smiled, a pleased gleam in his Dalton blue eyes that were so like her own. Roni realized he'd already planned the wedding in his mind and all that was left was the formality of the ceremony. All her love for him rushed to the surface. She gave him a fierce hug.

"We'll get Marta to make the cake," he continued. "The roses are in bloom. Amelia puts a pretty bouquet together. Or would you rather have an orchid from the florist?"

"Roses," Roni said. Her knees went a little weak. She studied Adam while he and her uncle made plans.

A bolt of fear sliced down her spine while her heart went delirious with joy. Adam was the man of her dreams, but sometimes dreams turned into nightmares. Marriage had never been part of his plans.

However, he'd always been protective and caring toward his little sister. He was acting the same toward her. Where there was caring, there was also love. Weren't they one and the same?

A tiny glow centered in her heart. "I'll have to see if Patricia can come," she told the two men who were determined to take over her life. "We promised to be each other's maid of honor."

"And you always keep your word," Adam murmured.

"If you're a Dalton, you do," Uncle Nick said, a firm warning in the words as he met Adam's eyes.

Adam smiled, his eyes on her, his expression sardonic once more. "It takes a braver man than I am to cross the Dalton gang," he said.

"You don't have to do this," Roni told Adam on Monday at noon. She'd been up since four that morning, working on the new project, and felt tired and disheveled.

"I think it's customary," he replied.

They'd met downtown at eleven and gone through the arrangements for the marriage license. She'd spoken to the pastor at the Lost Valley church and to Marta, who was the church pianist and who would also make the cake.

Amelia and the other Dalton wives would take care of the flowers and food for the reception at the newly completed lodge next to the lake. Later there would be a dinner for the family and close friends. She and Adam would then retire to their honeymoon suite on the second floor.

Everything was under control. All she had to do was relax and enjoy. Right?

Adam held the door to the jewelry store. She went inside, with him close behind, as if to cut off any escape attempts on her part. But there was no backing out. She'd given her word.

"May I help you?" the woman behind the counter asked, giving them a bright, expectant smile.

"We need wedding bands," Adam explained. "And an engagement ring. A diamond one."

"No, no." Roni shook her head. "There's no need to waste money on a diamond."

"What would you rather have?" he asked.

"Nothing. I mean, you don't have to get an engagement ring. I'll hardly have time to wear it before we're…before the…"

"Ceremony?" he supplied. "We have the rest of the week. Besides, your uncle will expect it. We'll look at the one carat diamonds," he said to the jeweler.

The woman visually measured her hand, then removed a black velvet tray filled with shining gold circles encrusted with sparkling diamonds. "Try one of these on," she invited.

Roni tried to pick the smallest and plainest of the rings on the tray. Adam selected one with a large diamond in the center and two sprays of smaller diamonds curving gracefully on each side. It wasn't the largest or most ornate, but Roni thought it the most beautiful.

When he slid it on, she had a selfish urge to close her hand into a fist so he couldn't change his mind and remove it. She resisted the impulse.

"Will this do?" he asked.

She tried to read the numbers on what was surely the smallest price tag in the world. "How much is it?" she asked the woman.

The store owner read the tag without hesitation.

"Bionic eyes," Adam murmured to Roni.

He gave her a conspiratorial grin when she gazed at

him in alarm at the cost. "That's too much." She tried to remove the ring.

His hand closed over hers. "She's very practical," he told the jeweler. "We'll take it."

"Would you like them engraved?" the owner asked. "Most couples put their initials inside the band. We can easily add a phrase—"

"No," Roni interrupted, unable to go that far.

She was silent while Adam's credit card was run through the machine. The sale was approved. He signed the credit slip and pocketed the white jewelry box that contained the matching wedding bands, each carved with curving leaf patterns that echoed the diamond sprays on the other ring.

If worst came to worst, she decided as they left amid the store owner's congratulations, she would repay him and keep the ring. She realized she was already thinking ahead to the end of their union, as if some part of her knew it wouldn't last.

"Seth says a person shouldn't use a credit card to charge large items," she told him once they were in the car. "Unless you pay the total balance each month."

"That's what I do." He gave her a glance as he stopped at a red light. "I'm not stupid with money," he assured her. "I'm not a miser, either."

"We can work out a budget. Without the rent on your apartment, we should be able to save more."

He made a sound which she took to be assent. On the

drive across town to a gourmet restaurant, she considered several plans and decided they could split all living expenses down the middle, then each should be able to save more. If there was a child, they would need to enlarge the house.

She had it all worked out by the time they arrived at the restaurant. Inside they were quickly seated. Within ten minutes they had been served drinks and had ordered.

"You're quiet," Adam mentioned once they were alone. He observed her over the rim of his iced-tea glass. "Which I find not only unusual but perhaps a bit alarming. About to change your mind about us?"

Roni shook her head. "It's too late. Things have gone too far." She flushed at his sharp glance.

"If you're adamantly opposed, we can call it off."

His tone was relaxed, perhaps amused. He'd been the same yesterday when they'd told the rest of the Daltons about their plans. No one had seemed surprised.

She frowned as the heat increased in her face. Had the hunger between them been so obvious?

Don't answer that, she told herself, then had to smile at how ridiculous she was.

"What?" he asked.

"Us. Marriage. Do you want a prenuptial agreement?" she asked, getting down to practical details.

He obviously hadn't considered it. With a shrug, he said, "I have an anemic IRA and enough in savings to get me through a year. And some secondhand furniture in the apartment. You're welcome to half."

She nodded. "The mortgage company owns most of the cottage, but a sliver belongs to me."

Adam chuckled.

After their salads were delivered, she explained that she'd accepted stock in lieu of a higher salary when she'd joined the start-up educational company and that she would get royalties on a game she'd developed.

"Games are something new for us. We just started those last year and will ship the first one soon. It may be a flop, one of those bubbles that'll burst in our faces. If it isn't, G-2 and I will get royalties. The reviews are coming in now and they seem to be favorable."

Adam nodded. "Sounds interesting. I have to admit I don't know much about how your business works." He looked thoughtful. "Maybe we should do the prenuptial to protect your assets."

"Well, for now they're mostly imaginary. It might be months before we know the full impact."

"In that case we probably won't need an agreement."

A chill rushed over her at his casual tone. Their eyes met, and they observed each other without speaking. She smiled when he did, but a premonition of disaster filled her. Adam obviously didn't have much faith in the marriage.

However, Uncle Nick had never let any of the orphans do things halfway. She would do her part. If the marriage failed, it wouldn't be her fault.

"Eat up," Adam advised when their food was delivered. "Greg is making his big leasing presentation this afternoon. At Geena's request, I'm sitting in as a consultant."

Roni glanced at the engagement ring. Its sparkle was just as bright, but the lighting in the restaurant seemed much dimmer.

"You're looking a little green," Patricia commented. "Are you thinking of calling it off?"

Roni wasn't surprised that her friend picked up on her thoughts. They'd shared many confidences over the years and understood each other very well. Roni had confided the events leading up to the wedding. "I can't."

Patricia nodded, her eyes on the road as they neared the turnoff to the ranch. Roni had ridden up with her friend on the theory that she would be returning to the city with Adam tomorrow and wouldn't need her own car.

"It's nice that everyone will be here," Patricia said in a musing tone. "With the lodge having its grand opening this weekend, this works out great, huh?"

"Yes."

"Don't get too enthused," her friend remarked dryly.

Roni sighed. "Now that the time has come, it's hard to know if we're doing the right thing."

"You are," Patricia said without a doubt in the world.

Strangely, Roni felt comforted by that.

"About time," her uncle greeted her in the huge lobby of the lodge when the two friends arrived.

The older man looked a bit frazzled, which increased

the apprehension Roni was trying to ignore. Adam had been remote all week, and her nights had been restless. She'd needed the reassurance of his arms, she realized.

Amelia came from the kitchen, saw her and dashed over to give her a hug and shake hands with Patricia after the introduction. "Your room is ready. So is the dress. Do you want to try it on?"

"Maybe you'd better," Patricia warned. "I think you've lost weight this week."

"I haven't," Roni denied, but she let her friends take charge and did as she was told without comment.

They led her to the room that would be the bridal suite after the wedding. The sitting room was pleasantly scented with pale yellow and pink roses, arranged in white baskets with flowing ribbons. Roni counted twelve of the bouquets.

"These will go to the church as soon as Seth and Beau get back. They're running errands."

After lunch in the suite, Roni paced from window to window, unable to settle down. She knew she should rest, but it was beyond her.

"We're going to take a walk," Patricia announced. "Put on your sneakers."

Roni and her friend went down the back stairway, found Marta and Amelia in the kitchen, along with the resort staff, informed the women of their plans, then headed out around the lake.

Their walk took them by the Victorian farm house Zack and Honey had bought last year. Roni told her friend of the couple's plans to make the place their home and about the coming child.

"You and Adam will need to enlarge your house when you have children," Patricia remarked.

Roni nodded, blinking back unexplainable tears.

"Roni? What is it?" Patricia peered at her. "I've never seen you so nervy."

"Bridal jitters," Roni assured her.

They walked for two hours. At the lodge, Patricia insisted that they rest before it was time to shower and dress. "I want to do your hair special, too," she said.

Later, a friend from high school, who had opened a photography shop in Lost Valley, took pictures during the dressing and hair arranging stages of preparation, then she rushed off to the church. Roni gave Patricia the groom's ring that Adam had left with her yesterday.

The bride and bridesmaid joined Uncle Nick and Seth in the sparkling clean station wagon. Someone had put a bouquet of ribbons on the antenna. Two police cruisers, their lights flashing, fell into place before and behind the ranch vehicle.

"Arranged by Zack," Seth told her, tossing a grin over his shoulder.

Roni took a deep breath and put a smile on her face as she waved to shopkeepers and clerks who came out of their stores to see the grand procession. Ranchers, in town for Saturday shopping, and total strangers, in town for a respite from the city, blew their horns enthusiastically.

Roni's spirits soared upward. It was a perfect day for

the wedding. What was not to like? she asked herself as they arrived at the small church she'd attended all her growing years.

She blinked at the number of vehicles in the parking lot. The attendance must be as large as the Easter Sunday crowd. Three television trucks were also there.

"Alison's parents were planning on coming up," Seth told them. "Looks as if the senator's campaign for governor is going strong."

"If they try to make this a three-ring circus, I'll throw them out," Uncle Nick assured Roni.

She and Patricia glanced at each in mock alarm, then grinned. "Daltons can handle anything," she told her favorite relative.

He was handsome in his dark blue Sunday suit. His thick white hair had a stubborn wave that fell over his forehead no matter how much he combed it to the side. A storm surge of love for this family icon rushed over her.

Amelia was there to help straighten their dresses while Seth went to warn the pastor and groom of the bride's arrival. Television cameras recorded the action.

From the open doors to the chapel, Roni heard the music that signaled the first of the wedding party to gather at the front of the church.

Amelia looked her over. "You have something borrowed, something blue?" she asked.

Roni surveyed her outfit. Her gown was a mellow cream color due to age. It and the veil were old. Her shoes, dyed to match, were new. Patricia had given her a set of blue garters. "I don't have anything borrowed."

Amelia removed a strand of pearls from her purse. "These were my grandmother's. She would be pleased to know they were being put to good use."

Again the sting of tears caused Roni to blink. She touched the pearls with trembling fingers after Amelia secured them around her neck. "Thank you."

Her new sister-in-law gave her arm a squeeze and hurried inside to take her place with Seth. Roni, Uncle Nick and Patricia entered the vestibule of the church.

She was surprised at the profusion of rose baskets that lined the worn wooden floor and the festoons of ribbons over the doorway. The Dalton clan had obviously been busy, all of it at their wives's instigation, Roni was sure.

At that moment, the twins, Travis and Trevor, swung open the double doors into the chapel.

Patricia checked that she had the gold band, then began her walk down the aisle. When she was in position, Marta segued into the bridal march.

Uncle Nick offered his arm. He and Roni began the journey that would take her into a new life.

White candles and roses stood in tiers on graceful candelabras around the front dais. Ferns formed a verdant backdrop. More white baskets of the pink and yellow roses marked the end of each pew. Rose petals and curling pieces of ribbon carpeted the white satin floor covering where she and Adam were to stand. She'd never seen the country church so lovely. Her friend took pictures of it all.

At last she stood beside Adam. Zack was in place as best man. Roni had been pleased when Adam had told her he planned to ask the deputy, who was also his brother-in-law, to fill the position.

"Dearly beloved," the pastor began, and proceeded through the traditional exchange of vows and rings. "You may kiss the bride," he intoned at the end.

Adam lifted the lace veil and pressed her lips in a gentle kiss. Then he did the same with her hand, placing the kiss on the wedding band. Electricity shot through her ring finger and zinged straight to her heart.

It came to her with unerring certainty that, whatever else the day might mean in years to come, whether joy or regret, she had married this man for love.

Only for love.

Chapter Eight

Roni glanced at the gold ring circling her finger and the matching one Adam wore. A married couple. They were truly a married couple. She wasn't sure she believed it.

Maybe tonight she would. Or surely by the morning.

A bolt of electricity ran through her as she and her very new husband went into the lodge. The dining room was as beautiful as the church. The three-tiered wedding cake held pride of place on a table covered in pink linen. The groom's cake, which was chocolate on the inside, was next to it.

The television crews had followed the party from the church. They were allowed to film the senator and his wife, who were invited because they were Alison's parents, as the older couple congratulated the bridal pair. Then the men were told to put away their cameras and join the feast.

Roni was greeted and kissed by people she didn't know. Seth explained that the lodge was almost full for the grand opening and he'd told the guests to join them for the wedding buffet since the restaurant wasn't available for other meals that evening.

Amid a laughing, noisy crowd, the couple ate, cut the cakes, received a dozen toasts and then led the first waltz when a local combo set up their instruments in an alcove of the room.

"Our first dance," she said to Adam, who was surprisingly good. She followed him effortlessly.

His eyes were appreciative as he perused her finery. "You're incredibly beautiful," he murmured.

"Thank you," she said demurely. A contented sigh escaped her. Maybe everything was going to be okay.

She tossed a bouquet of ribbons and roses that matched her bridal bouquet, then Adam removed one of the blue garters from under her skirt, taking a lot of teasing as he did so, and tossed it into the crowd.

There was laughter when Trevor, the last Dalton bachelor, caught it. He smiled good-naturedly as he held the trophy up so everyone could see, then tucked it in his pocket. Later, he returned it to Adam.

At nine o'clock, Adam asked if she was ready to leave. That meant going up the stairs to their suite. Her heart did its fluttery thing as she nodded. She kissed Uncle Nick and thanked him for being wonderful, then she thanked everyone who'd helped arrange the wedding on such short notice.

Adam waited patiently at her side until she finished. When the couple started to leave, the male Daltons formed an honor guard to the steps, then closed ranks behind them so that no overly exuberant guests could follow.

In their quarters, Adam locked the door behind them, then watched as she laid aside her flowers, then the veil of Holland lace her grandmother had once worn. Leaving her satin shoes beside the table, she noted the silver bucket filled with ice and a private bottle of champagne. A silver tray of fruit, crackers and cheese had been provided.

"Hungry?" he asked, following her gaze.

"No." She waited for him to come to her, to take her into his arms and get them past this strained moment and the return of her earlier anxiety and uncertainty.

He nodded, then took off his jacket and tie and placed them over a chair. He studied her thoughtfully.

"I…I'll go get dressed…undressed. Uh, I'll change…" She rushed toward the bedroom before her dignity cracked completely.

"Wait. I have something to discuss with you."

She stopped in mid-flight.

"This is rather awkward." He smiled slightly and came toward her. He stopped a good three feet away, his hands in his pockets. "Due to the circumstances, I felt we had to proceed with the marriage."

When he paused as if expecting some reaction from her, she nodded.

"But there's no need to compound the error," he continued in the same thoughtful manner. "I've considered our options over this past week and I think this is the best path to take."

"What path?" she asked, not getting the point of the discussion at all.

"If there's no child, we'll stay together for perhaps six months. I'll finish the case by then and ask for reassignment elsewhere, then we can separate and say the marriage didn't work out. We'll get an annulment."

"How can we get an annulment?" she asked, her mind grappling furiously with this new situation.

"If we don't…sleep together," he said, putting it delicately, "then we can swear we haven't consummated the marriage and ask for an annulment."

Slowly enlightenment dawned. "Then why did we get married?"

"In case of a child foremost. And to appease your uncle. I know you value his opinion. This way he'll know we've given it a shot and it didn't work." Adam shrugged. "We'll split, no harm done."

The shock of it nearly rendered her speechless. "Let me get this straight," she said slowly. "It was okay for us to *sleep* together before we were married, but now that we are married, we're going to be platonic?"

He shot her a frown. "Yes."

She couldn't help it; she started to laugh. "It'll never work."

"It will. We'll just have to exercise some self-control."

"You exercise whatever you want," she told him. She stepped into the bedroom, her grand exit line ready. "It'll take a divorce to get rid of me."

She slammed the door and locked it for good measure. Then she pressed her ear to the wood.

Not a sound could be heard from the other side. After two eternal minutes, she concluded he wasn't going to pound on the door and demand that she open it at once.

Which she'd been prepared to do.

"Well," she said to the empty bed, not sure what to do now that her bluff hadn't worked. All her doubts returned.

She removed the wedding dress and satin petticoat, the white stockings and garter belt woven with pink roses, the blue garter that matched the one thrown to the bachelors, the low-cut silk bra with its sexy front closure.

From her suitcase, she lifted the pink negligee set the other Dalton brides had presented to her for tonight. It was the loveliest thing she'd ever owned, a froth of silk and lace that hinted at what was underneath without actually quite disclosing anything. It was meant to drive the groom wild.

Looking at herself in the full-length mirror on the bathroom door, she sighed as she recalled all the foolish dreams she'd had of this night during the past week, then she narrowed her eyes at her image.

"You can run," she warned the absent bridegroom, "but can you hide?"

She considered the six months Adam had declared they should give the marriage if parenthood didn't materialize. At the end of that time, they would see who called it quits.

It wouldn't be her.

As usual, Roni woke at the crack of dawn. She yawned and stretched in the queen-size bed, then headed for the bathroom to prepare for the day. After she was dressed, she considered what to do.

Go back to the city, she decided. She wasn't up to facing any of her family today and acting the delirious blushing bride. Standing by the window, she tried to figure out exactly how she did feel.

Dismayed more than despairing, she concluded. Tired. Angry. Frustrated. There was perhaps a bit of resentment at Adam's high-handed manner, his determination not to give her or their marriage a chance.

Not a happy camper, she noted, catching her solemn image in the mirror. She tried to smile and put things in perspective, but her spirits weren't up to it.

She packed her weekend case and replaced the wedding outfit in its plastic bag and tucked the pearls in an envelope addressed to Amelia.

After pausing to build up her courage, she opened the door to the living room. Adam was asleep on the sofa, his head on one end, his feet dangling over the other. He looked uncomfortable. Served him right.

He'd changed to jeans and T-shirt. His suitcase stood ready near the door, as if he'd planned a quick getaway, then had gone to sleep instead. He opened his eyes.

"Leaving?" he asked.

She nodded. "I'd like to go home. To the city."

He sat upright, pulled on his boots and stood. "Without seeing your relatives?"

"Yes."

He gave her a sharp perusal, but she simply returned his gaze without comment. Her mixed emotions coalesced into a solid lump in her chest. Like the mountain peaks, he appealed to her heart, but also like them, he was remote and forbidding. Avoiding the wedding dress, he took her case, then picked up his own bag.

Carrying the bouquet and dress, she followed him down the steps. A clerk was already behind the reception desk. She kept giving Roni peculiar glances as Roni asked her to explain to the Dalton relatives that she and Adam needed to return to the city that morning.

Roni hurried outside. Adam waited at the curb in front of the lodge. He leaned over and opened the door for her.

"I need to stop by Amelia's place," she said.

The three-minute trip was accomplished in dead silence. He stopped at the Victorian on the other side of town. Roni leaped out and rushed up the steps. Inside she found Amelia in the kitchen as expected.

"Well, good morning," her sister-in-law said in surprise. "You're up early."

"Adam and I are heading back to Boise. I wanted to return these and thank you for letting me wear them. That was so nice of you." She handed over the pearls.

Amelia slid the envelope into her apron pocket. "They were perfect with your outfit." She glanced past Roni. "Uh, why don't you and Adam come in and have breakfast with us? Seth is getting dressed. He'll be here in a minute."

"Thanks, but I'm working on a new project—"

Roni stopped abruptly as she realized how that sounded, as if a new bride would be itching to get back to work.

"Is everything okay?" Amelia asked gently.

Roni nodded, then shook her head. "I don't think I understand men, which seems odd considering I grew up in a house filled with them." Her smile wasn't very successful.

Amelia poured a cup of coffee and handed it to Roni, then took a seat on a stool by the counter where a cup of tea cooled. "Men can be boneheaded," she said, "Seth and Adam more than most, I think." She added honey and took a sip of the tea. "Seth didn't think he could ever marry because he didn't have a right to the Dalton name."

Roni was surprised at this. As they now knew, Seth was not a blood relative, but when Uncle Nick had taken the orphans in, they'd thought he was. It was all straightened out now and Seth was part of the family.

"How silly. Of course he does. The family would be lost without him. Besides, we love him. He'll always seem like a brother to me."

"I think he finally understands that." Amelia raised her eyebrows in question. "What's Adam's problem?"

"He doesn't want to be married."

Amelia sat back in her chair, stunned. "So why did he go through with it?"

"His sense of responsibility. There could be a child." Roni hesitated, uncomfortable. "Last night Adam said we could get the marriage annulled if there's no baby and we don't sleep together. So he slept on the couch."

"The louse." Amelia looked as if she would like to go outside and confront the bridegroom on the spot.

"That's what I thought, too." Roni sighed. "I'm not sure what to do next."

"Seduce him," Amelia advised dryly. "Tell him he'll have to get a divorce if he wants to get rid of you."

"I told him that. It was my grand exit line last night, right before I slammed and locked the bedroom door."

Amelia pressed a hand to her mouth as a chortle escaped her. "Good for you. Look, if he tries any of that platonic stuff when you get home, tell him that was his idea, not yours. Drive him crazy. He's bound to crack soon."

"But…is that fair?"

"Adam may have a problem with commitment. He and Honey were abandoned by their parents in the sense that their dad was killed and their mom died when they were young. Adam might be afraid to love. Except for his sister, of course." Amelia lightly touched Roni's shoulder. "I've seen the way he's looked at you a couple of times at the ranch. The fact that he rushed into marriage to protect you from Uncle Nick's wrath is significant, too. I think subconsciously he wants the marriage, but he can't admit that. It makes him too vulnerable."

She slipped on oven mitts and removed a pan of muffins from the oven. After placing them on top of the stove, she resumed her seat.

"Who's vulnerable?" Seth asked, coming into the kitchen and giving his wife a smooch on the neck. He ruffled Roni's bangs. "Mmm, those muffins smell delicious. Are they about ready?"

"You're vulnerable if you touch those," she warned. "They're for Roni and Adam to take home with them."

Seth looked his sister over. "What's happening?"

"Nothing," Roni quickly said.

"They're on their way back to the city," Amelia explained. She boxed up a variety of muffins and a loaf of banana nut bread, placed the box beside Roni, added two insulated containers of coffee, then handed Seth a plate with two hot muffins and a pat of butter. She grinned at him. He grinned back.

Roni felt her heart contract at the easy affection between the other two. "I'd better go. Adam is probably wondering if he should send out a search party."

"I was," a masculine voice spoke behind her. "But I decided I had better check on my runaway bride myself."

Roni met her brother's quick glance with a stoic smile. "I'm not going to run away," she assured Adam, a hint of determination running through the humorous tone. "Amelia, thoughtful as usual, fixed us a box of goodies to take with us. The banana nut bread is mine," she declared. She hugged her brother and sister-in-law. "We'd best be off. I really do have a ton of work to do this next week. Thanks for all your help on the wedding, and for the treats."

After she and Adam were on the highway, she gave him a muffin and took one for herself. They ate, sipped the coffee, then endured the rest of the trip to the city in silence, without trying to make small talk.

At the cottage, he carried in her bag and the box of food while she handled the bouquet and wedding dress.

"Well," he said.

She detected a farewell in the word and spoke before he could continue. "How long will it take for you to move your things over here?"

"I don't think—"

"You can have the bedroom. I'll move my things to the office. I have a daybed in there." She'd thought all this out while they were on the road.

"I'm not taking your bedroom," he told her.

She frowned. "I think it'll be easier to move my clothing than my desk and computer equipment. But if you want the other room—"

"I don't want either room," he said in a near growl.

"What do you want?" she asked in the same vein.

A long silence ensued.

At last he rammed his hands in his pockets and paced the living room. "I thought I would keep my place."

"Oh, fine. That'll really convince my uncle we gave the marriage a real try."

He huffed and paced some more. "All right. I'll move in here. For six months."

She nodded. "Help me move my stuff, then we'll go over to your place and pack up."

"I can handle it. I'll have to figure out what to do with the furniture," he said, planning the details. "For now, I'll collect what I need and bring it over here."

"There's a storage shed behind the house. We can put some stuff in there."

His dark countenance didn't invite more comment. She marched to her office, tossed the wedding gown and bouquet on the daybed, then went to her bedroom and began removing clothes from the closet.

From the other room, she heard Adam's footsteps, then the sound of a door closing. She rushed to the front window in time to see him drive off.

She stood there for a minute, then sank into a chair, her heart dropping to her toes. She wondered if he really planned to return, or if upon reaching his home he would decide to stay there. Then she noticed the suitcase with his wedding clothing sitting inside the door.

Adam parked in the narrow driveway and sat in the car while he surveyed the cottage and its riot of flowers. It looked like something out of a fairy tale.

In one such story, a witch had lived inside, one who ate little boys and girls.

Don't get carried away, he advised his morbid imagination. Roni was far from being a witch, and that was the problem. He might die from sheer frustration at having to live in the same house while keeping his hands off her.

It would be difficult, but he would survive. He had to think of her and what was best. As he should have done last weekend when he'd been weak and given in to passion.

His body reacted to the memories. "Six months," he muttered. "The gods must be laughing."

He stacked a couple of boxes and carried them inside. There he found Roni at her computer. She told him the other room was ready. He went into the bedroom vacated for him.

The dresser drawers were empty. He stored his socks and underwear in two of them. That left four drawers. He retrieved his suits and placed them in the closet, using half the space. After storing his empty luggage on the top shelf, he noticed the wedding dress tucked into the other side.

His heart turned a few flips as he recalled how she'd looked, coming down the aisle on her uncle's arm, both of them solemn and reserved. When she'd met his eyes, she'd smiled. In that instant, she'd been the radiant bride...*his* radiant bride...and for that moment he'd believed it was possible, that she could be his and they would live in the storybook happily-ever-after paradise forever.

Then reality had set in. He knew that nothing good ever lasted very long. Not for him at any rate. For each person, life had its patterns, and they were difficult or impossible to break. He'd learned that a long time ago.

That was the reason he'd been adamant about his little sister fulfilling her dream of being a dancer. He'd wanted her life to follow a different path, one of success and happiness, of expectations and fulfillment, so he'd stayed out of her way.

Even that had nearly failed when the danger of his work spilled over into her life. They'd gotten the two men who'd tried to kill her, but he might not be so lucky next time.

If some thugs tried to hurt Roni, he'd tear them apart with his bare hands, protect her with his last breath…

He shook his head. Man, how morbid could he get?

Unzipping the protective covering, he reached inside and touched the smooth satin of the wedding dress, then jerked back in surprise. It was warm to his touch, as if she'd taken it off less than a minute ago.

He ran a fingertip over the ruffle of lace that had lain against the sweet curve of her bosom. Longing erupted, filling him with needs so powerful he could hardly breathe. He clutched a fistful of lace and closed his eyes until the painful spasm eased.

"All this," he muttered. All this because of one small woman and the hunger she unleashed in him.

"Is that in your way?" a voice inquired.

He let go of the material and zipped the cover closed before facing her. "No," he said, his voice husky. He cleared his throat. "I was wondering if you needed some room. I won't use more than half this space."

"I'm fine. Patti helped me go through my stuff when I moved here. She threw out all my old jeans that were too ragged to wear anymore." She sighed loudly. "It was like throwing away old friends."

Her wry smile drove the odd shaft of pain through him again. He wondered if this was a foretaste of the next six months. If so, it wouldn't be long before he exploded into bits and pieces.

"What else have you got?" she asked. "I'll help."

Ignoring his protests, she carried in eight wire baskets filled with jeans and casual clothing and stored them in the two support racks he snapped together and placed in the closet under the suits and white shirts.

One large plastic bin held his shoes. He put it on the floor next to the wedding dress. Roni looked it over.

"Ski boots. Several pairs of jogging and tennis shoes. Golfing shoes." She wrinkled her nose at those, then laughed and shook her head.

He knew she was recalling her disastrous day on the golf course with Geena and Scott.

"Hiking and working boots. Uncle Nick likes that brand of work boot," she told him, then continued the inventory. "The boots you wear at the ranch. One pair of fancy cowboy boots. They're dusty. You don't wear them often."

"They were a stupid buy."

"Maybe not. The Dalton men have dude boots. They

used to wear them to dances to impress the girls." She gave him an oblique perusal. "You lead an active life, Special Agent Smith," she said softly.

He liked the approval in her tone and the smile in her eyes when she glanced at him. He liked lots of things about her…too much. His body surged with unappeased hunger.

He turned and headed back to the car to get the box of toiletries he'd taken from the medicine chest before she had a chance to notice the very evident ridge straining against his pants zipper.

It had taken him a long time to get to sleep last night due to the same tension in his body. He'd wanted to go to her, to take all the promise in her eyes and the passion in that slender but strong body.

But he hadn't. There was no use adding complications to an otherwise simple situation. In six months, or less if all went well, he'd leave and that would be the end of it. Satisfied with this logic, he went into the cottage.

She was in the kitchen. "Chicken salad sandwiches okay for lunch?"

His first impulse was to tell her he'd go out someplace to eat, but that didn't seem polite. "Uh, yes."

"There's an empty medicine chest in the bathroom," she told him as she laid out four slices of whole wheat bread.

In the bathroom he found two sinks, a shower and, in an alcove, a commode with a handy basket of magazines in one corner. He opened a medicine cabinet door over the nearest sink. Her scent wafted around him.

The cabinet was filled with her things—toothbrushes, toothpaste, bottles of perfume, body powder and deodorant, aspirin, vitamins and cold capsules.

He quickly closed the door, feeling guilty at invading her space, and stored his few items in the matching medicine chest over the other sink.

"Towels and washcloths in the double doors under the sinks," she called out. "I spray the walls and floor of the shower each time I use it."

He spotted the spray bottle of cleanser sitting in a niche in the wall along with shampoo, conditioner and soap. The intimacy of sharing a house with her struck him.

"Lunch," she announced.

He took the empty box to the kitchen. "Where can I put this?"

"Trash and recycle stuff goes under here." She opened a door to show him, then opened other cabinets and drawers. "Glasses. Plates. Bowls. Silverware."

After disclosing the contents of the kitchen, she took her place on a stool at the island counter. He joined her, his knee accidentally brushing her leg as he sat on the high stool next to her. "Sorry."

"S'okay," she mumbled around a mouthful of sandwich.

On each plate was a variety of fresh veggies—carrots, radishes, cucumbers, jicama, plus slices of Asian pear and several strawberries. The chicken salad sandwiches had been grilled, something new to him. Tall glasses of iced tea accompanied the meal.

"Mmm, delicious," he said after the first bite of the sandwich.

"This was one of my dad's favorite meals."

"You remember him?"

"Some things. He was great fun. He and my uncle were identical twins, like Travis and Trevor. Wouldn't it be neat if Zack and Honey had twins?"

Adam wasn't thinking of his sister, but of the woman beside him as he considered the impact of twins on a person's life. Double trouble? Or double love?

He frowned at the second thought. He didn't know where these sentimental ideas were coming from. Tomorrow, when he went back to work, everything would be normal again, he assured his doubtful, perplexed self.

"What are you thinking?" she asked softly.

"Of work," he said truthfully.

She blinked once. Her expression changed from dreamy pleasure to an unreadable mask.

He knew—somehow he knew—that he'd hurt her. He searched for words to soothe her, to explain what he'd meant, then realized it was best to keep a cool distance between them. He couldn't be careful of her feelings every minute.

For the rest of the silent meal, he could have been eating cardboard.

After she finished, she stored her dishes in the dishwasher, then she went to the quilting frame, taking her stool to perch on. She slipped a thimble on a finger, then lifted the needle and proceeded to stitch the golden thread into the material. The surprise must have shown on his face.

"Did you think this was only for looks, like those fancy homes with baby grand pianos that no one can play?"

He nodded and finished the last bite of his sandwich and ate the last strawberry. Following her example, he put the plate in the dishwasher and refilled his tea glass.

Seeing a coaster on the quilting frame, he refilled her glass and took it to her.

"Thanks."

He lingered, his gaze on the colored squares in the quilt. "I think I've read that quilt designs have names, but I don't recall what they were."

"This is a simple starburst pattern with a twist. I used light and dark squares to make each larger square so that it forms a tick tack toe grid. I then add two red and one yellow circle as if the game is in progress. In the very center, I'll stitch a completed set with red as the winner."

"Maybe we should play to see who wins."

She laughed and shook her head. "This is my quilt. I'll decide the winner."

He settled on the chenille sofa and found it very comfortable. A yawn overcame him and he realized he was sleepy.

"Take your shoes off and stretch out," she invited. "I don't have any rules against propping your feet on the furniture. Comfort is the key in this household."

"Good thinking."

He sipped the chilled tea and watched her work, her

fingers fast and skillful as she sewed the tiny stitches. It came to him that she was very creative, designing computer games and lessons, making quilts, creating a home in the tiny cottage that could rival the mansion they'd visited two weekends ago.

Whoa, he cautioned. It was true she was smart, talented and beautiful, but she wasn't for him. He had to keep that in the forefront of his mind during the next few months.

He slid down on the sofa, then realized he was too drowsy to sit upright. Taking her advice, he pulled his legs up and stretched out full length, pleased to discover that his feet didn't hang off the end. This was the most comfortable sofa he'd ever found, much better than the short one at the lodge last night. He yawned. His eyes slid closed and refused to open.

From a distance, he heard soft noises. He opened his eyes a slit. Roni closed another curtain, then settled in the easy chair. She flipped a lever, turning it into a recliner, then closed her eyes.

A smile tugged at his mouth. His idea of sleeping with a woman didn't involve him on a couch and her on a chair.

A vision of the night spent in her bed swept over him, bringing the heat and the hardness that he'd come to expect whenever he recalled those hours they'd really and truly slept together.

Someplace inside him a vortex gathered and spun furiously around a black void, a place of emptiness he'd always been able to ignore. Until he'd slept with *her*.

Life could be like that, a vast circular yearning for things that could never be. He'd learned not to want too much. His last thought was to worry about where the passion between him and the woman who slept peacefully in his presence would lead.

Chapter Nine

Roni and Patricia occupied their favorite table at their favorite restaurant the following Friday.

"I can't believe the last day of May is tomorrow," Roni said, studying the calendar on the screen of her personal digital assistant, which contained her schedule, any bright ideas that came to her and other important stuff she had to keep track of. She turned off the PDA and stored it in her purse. "So much has happened since the month began."

"I'll say," Patricia chimed in. "Life is a game of dominoes. Who knew on the first Friday when you crashed into Adam's table that you would start a chain of events that would lead to your being an old married lady by the last Friday of the month?"

"A week hardly counts as 'old,'" Roni informed her best friend. "It only seems forever," she finished wryly.

"Still platonic?"

Roni nodded.

"I'd be climbing the walls by now."

The bride managed a smile. "I'll survive."

Actually she'd been working from early in the morning until late at night on the new computer game. She and her co-worker, G-2, were creating puzzles for Merinda, their heroine, to solve. The girl's name came from the fact that they had decided she could change from human to mermaid form with the help of a magic necklace that she had to charm away from an old sea serpent.

The work was absorbing, and she put in longer hours than usual so she wouldn't have to think about her odd marriage and the fact that her groom showed up around ten o'clock each night, just in time to go to bed, and left at the crack of dawn each morning. She rarely saw him.

"Uh-oh," Patricia murmured.

Roni glanced over her shoulder. Adam was threading his way between tables. He stopped at theirs.

"Ladies." He nodded his head to each of them, then looked at her. "I, uh, need to check with you on something for this weekend."

"Yes?"

"We're invited to a dinner tomorrow night. Are you avail—" He glanced at Patricia and obviously decided to reword the question. "Do we have any social obligations?"

"That's okay. Patricia knows all," Roni told him. She dug out the PDA and checked, knowing she had nothing but work scheduled for the weekend. "Nope. I'm free as a bird."

"Good."

"Is this with Geena and friends?" she asked, posing the stylus to insert the information on the screen.

"With CTC. Her father invited us. It's in the private dining room at the company headquarters at seven. Geena and Scott, also Greg Williams, will be there as well as other officers of the company."

Roni noted the time and again put the PDA in her purse. She looked up with a smile, expecting him to leave now that he'd delivered his message. He stood there as if waiting for something from her. Nothing came to mind.

"Uh, would you care to join us?" Patricia asked.

"Thanks." He pulled out a chair. "I haven't had lunch yet. What's good?"

"The salmon," Patricia told him.

When the waiter came over, that was what he ordered. Roni was surprised that he stayed after the way he'd been absent all week. She'd assumed that was the tone he'd decided to set for them, one of total avoidance.

While he and Patricia chatted about food and their favorite dishes, Roni wondered if she should leave. Her heart had gone all tight and fluttery when he joined them, but now she felt as if she might burst into tears. Where had her enthusiasm for life gone, her certainty that if she only worked hard enough all would be right with the world?

She sighed.

The other two paused.

"Are we celebrating anything tomorrow night?" she asked to fill the sudden silence.

"The company got a new contract."

"Great."

Unable to come up with casual conversation, she lapsed into almost total silence while she finished her meal, then waited for Adam while he ate, feeling it would be rude to leave, besides being odd for a bride to walk out and leave her new husband with another woman. Marriage introduced a lot of complications in one's life.

Patricia stood. "I have a two o'clock appointment," she told them, counting out money for her part of the bill.

"I'll get it," Adam said gallantly.

She smiled and shook her head. "Roni and I agreed long ago that a weekly luncheon together would be our treat to ourselves. We each pay our share so we don't have to remember who paid last." She left the money and departed.

"No wonder you two get along," Adam muttered. "She's as independent as you are."

"Women have had to be," Roni told him, rising to the defense of her sex. "Men vow forever, then leave us to raise the children alone while they go their merry ways."

He ate in silence for a bit, then asked, "Did that happen to someone you know?"

"As a matter of fact, it did. One of the secretaries at

work. Her husband left with another woman. She has three children to care for. Patricia and I were talking about it before you came."

"Before I butted in." He smiled slightly.

"We were glad to have you join us," she told him, being polite, then realized she was happy to see him. "Really," she added softly.

He nodded as he pushed the plate to the side and pulled the coffee cup closer. "You would tell me if you were pregnant, wouldn't you?"

She tried to figure out the undertone of worry. And why he was dwelling on it. A reason came to her. "Afraid you won't be able to hold out six months?" she teased, giving him a sexy glance from under her lashes.

His chest lifted and fell in a deep breath. "Don't push it," he warned.

"Maybe I want to."

She refused to back down from the latent anger that flashed through his eyes as he glared at her. His expression softened fractionally.

"Remember our agreement," he said. "We want a clean break when the time comes."

"That's what *you* want."

Now he frowned openly. Leaning close, he asked, "So what do you want?"

"We made vows, Adam. For better, for worse, through sickness and health. We promised to love, honor and cherish. Then we sealed those vows with a kiss. Did you have your fingers crossed all that time?"

His scowl deepened as if he was trying to figure out how to answer a trick question.

"Don't you remember King's X?" she asked. "When we were kids, we crossed our fingers to indicate we were out of the game at that moment and couldn't be tagged or whatever."

She held up both hands, index and middle fingers crossed to show him. It came to her that Adam's childhood had stopped when his mother had died and he and his sister went to live with their aunt.

Again she had that odd rush of tears. Again she forced it at bay. Adam would hate it if she showed pity for him.

She dropped her hands to her lap. "Sometimes, life won't let you take a 'time out' from living," she told him very gently. "We are truly married, whether you want it or not. And it was consummated, although the order was reversed." She hesitated. "But there is no child," she said softly, feeling the emptiness inside.

His eyes jerked to hers. "When did you know?"

"This morning. I would have told you, but you were gone when I got up." She stood. "You said we would give it six months, Adam, then talk about what comes next, whether a divorce or an annulment. Is that still the deal?"

He nodded, his gaze zeroing in on her waist.

Dropping a twenty dollar bill on the table, she left, her head high, her dignity intact. She hoped no one noticed how shaky her legs were.

* * *

The next morning Roni found Adam already up when she went into the kitchen. "Good morning," she said in the cheeriest voice possible, determined to be pleasant.

He looked up from the paper. "Good morning."

She prepared a bowl of nonfat yogurt, cereal and strawberries and sat at the island counter.

"I have to clear the rest of my stuff from the apartment," he told her. "It's the last day of the month, so I have to vacate. I've rented a truck."

Nothing like letting it go to the last possible moment, she thought, but refrained from voicing the sentiment. "Do you need any help?"

He hesitated so long she thought he was going to refuse. "As a matter of fact, if you'd drive me down to get the truck, I won't have to leave my car on the street."

"I'll be ready in ten minutes," she said and quickly ate, then poured coffee into a travel mug. "Okay."

He laid the paper aside. "I've never known a woman who actually took less time than she said she would."

She laughed. "In the Dalton household, if you were longer than five minutes in the shower, somebody turned the hot water off at the tank. I learned to be quick."

To her amazement, he looked annoyed.

"What's wrong?" she demanded, following him out of the cottage to his car. She got in the passenger side when he held the door for her.

"You," he said. He got in and backed out of the drive.

Roni waved to the old couple next door. They were already working amongst their flowers. "What about me?" she asked, turning to Adam.

"You don't hog the bathroom. You don't make noise. You don't leave clothes all over the house."

"And this makes you angry?"

"It's worrisome," he admitted, heading down the street, "like waiting for the other shoe to drop. You're too perfect. I know something is going to snap one of these days and all hell will break loose."

She laughed at his exaggerated frown. "You're pretty easy to live with, too. When you're not angry with me. Or eyeing me with suspicion. Or denying there's a mad passion between us while your eyes devour me."

He shot her an oblique, suspicious glance.

"Actually, we're a good fit," she continued. "We're both morning people. I nearly went insane waiting for Scott that weekend at his house."

"Huh."

"We're both neat." Another thought came to her. "Or are you just being nice for the duration?" Before he could answer, she added, "I suppose anyone can be nice for six months. Am I seeing the real you or are you actually a slob in neatnik's clothing?"

"Time will tell."

His sinister chuckle made her laugh. Still smiling, she relaxed and sipped the hot coffee while he turned down a narrow dirt lane that was potholed and rough. Gullies ran along each side of the road, leaving no space for parking a car. They passed a junkyard, a recycling place and arrived at the truck rental company.

"Nice neighborhood," she murmured. "I see why you didn't want to leave your car."

After he finished the details of the rental, Roni followed him from the area, then stayed behind him until he stopped under a portico beside a modern apartment building, its grounds artfully landscaped around a central pond.

She accompanied him to a service elevator. He gave her a quizzical glance, but didn't tell her to wait outside.

His apartment was on the second floor with a view toward the pond. It had an open floor plan with kitchen, dining and living room combined, plus a bedroom, study, a master bathroom and a powder room.

"Nice," she said.

"The furniture in here is rented. It'll be picked up this afternoon."

When he went into the bedroom, she peered into the study and found it empty, then trailed after him. His lack of furnishings reminded her of a man who lived life on the run, with few encumbrances to tie him down.

Such as a wife. Especially not a wife.

"This isn't secondhand," she said, gazing at the walnut armoire, matching dresser and a wonderful four-poster bed with burl wood inset into the headboard. "It's antique."

"I found it at a garage sale. It had been stored in a leaky barn for years. I refinished it."

She ran a hand over the dresser. The wood was as smooth as satin. "You did a wonderful job. This is beautiful."

When he started removing the drawers of the dresser, she pitched in and helped. After he wrapped each piece of the bedroom set in padding or blankets, she helped him cart them outside, then onto the hydraulic lift of the truck. The mattress and springs looked new and expensive.

He secured the furniture inside the truck with cords. Using the dolly that came with the rental, he wheeled out the television, then boxes containing linens, dishes and computer equipment. The last was a guitar.

"You play?" she asked in surprise.

"My father's."

His tone was so repressive, she stilled other questions that came to mind. After checking the apartment, he locked the door and left the key with the manager. She followed him home and helped unload, placing the guitar in a corner near the quilt. She imagined him playing it while she sewed.

They brought in his bedroom furniture. "This is so much better than anything I have," she said with a worried frown. "Let's put it in the house and store mine in the shed."

He considered, then nodded.

Pleased, she helped him get everything moved, then she tried a couple of different arrangements of his furniture before she was satisfied.

"This really belongs in an elegant Victorian," she

told him when they were finished. She leaned against the door frame, panting from the effort of shifting the heavy pieces.

Adam, she noted, was also breathing hard. He gave her an unexpected smile. "I've been thinking about a house that needs a lot of fixing up. I always thought I'd like to do a restoration."

"Sounds like fun. Zack and Honey plan to start on that old place they bought last year now that the resort is finished." She gestured toward the bare mattress. "Let's get the bed made up," she suggested and heard the huskiness that had invaded her voice.

He gave her a sharp glance, but didn't argue.

Together they tucked white sheets with lace edging over the mattress, then laid a comforter on top. She'd made the comforter using squares of material filled with pink roses interspersed with light green squares that depicted a white trellis with dark green ivy climbing on it. She'd also made matching pillow shams.

"Why do women use all these pillows nowadays?" he asked, a lazy, teasing smile on his face as he followed her example of leaning the lacy pillows against the headboard, then propping the sham-covered pillows against them, then adding the two small throw pillows in front.

"For color or texture. It makes a bedroom seem elegant and luxurious, I think."

She smiled at him across the broad bed, but he was no longer smiling. His gaze moved from the bed to her, then back to the bed, then again to her. Excitement rushed through her like a sudden wind off He-Devil peak.

Her breath quickened while heat formed a ball deep within. She knew the flames leaping in his eyes were reflected in her own. Need was a sudden, hot poignancy that dipped down to her soul, filling her with longing to share, really share, life with him.

He licked his lips and slightly shook his head, as if denying something that only he comprehended. "Come on. It's time to get the truck back."

The tension eased. Feeling carefree and oddly happy, she again drove behind him and waited while he returned the truck. This, she thought, was how a marriage could be if two people worked together. Why couldn't it be this way for her and Adam all the time?

It could. If he loved her. If he would let himself trust that love. If he would trust her love.

By shifting things in the closet, Adam managed to set up the computer credenza in it. With the laptop, printer and scanner in place, he only needed to add a phone line and he would be in business. With the chore of moving behind him, he let curiosity rule and went outside. He'd heard Roni go out earlier.

She was weeding along the back fence. The old man from next door was leaning on the side fence and talking to her.

"So," the elderly black man said, catching sight of him, "is this the new husband?"

Roni stood and turned. "Yes," she said, a smile in her voice, "that's him. Adam, I'd like you to meet Fred Twarp, a wonderful neighbor who looks after the cottage when I'm at the ranch, and me, when I'm home. He scolds if I neglect the roses. Fred, this is Adam Smith. His sister is married to my cousin."

"So that's how you met, eh?" Fred held a hand out.

"Yes." Adam went to the fence to shake hands. "Glad to meet you," he said. He nodded toward Roni. "It's good to know there's someone nearby to help keep an eye on her."

She huffed and rolled her eyes.

Fred chortled. It sounded like the dying gasp of a hoarse frog. "My wife's been worried about Roni working late at night," he confided to Adam, "but when we found out about the marriage, well, we decided those late hours might not be all work." He croaked and gasped some more.

Roni's soft giggle joined in. Adam had to grin.

"What's all this merriment?" a woman called out, "I thought you were out here working, Fred."

"My wife, Ethel." The older man introduced the frail but frisky woman who joined them. "We're the original Fred and Ethel," he joked. "The television couple was fashioned on us."

"Actually, I've always thought he was more like Valentino. He swept me off my feet," the wife said with a flirty glance at her husband.

"They eloped on their third date," Roni told him.

Listening to the older couple, Adam experienced a painful tightening in his chest. He wondered how anyone made it through a lifetime with one person.

With hard work and determination. With laughter and good humor. And sexy teasing that kept the flames ignited.

Roni asked a question about the roses. She pulled a few more weeds while Fred and Ethel argued over the best method to discourage the deer from eating all the blossoms. After the couple finished with their advice, they went inside for an afternoon nap.

Fred's eyes twinkled as he expounded on the merits of this habit. His croaky laughter followed him inside.

Roni pushed a wisp of hair out of her eyes. "I'm going for a run. There's a path through the woods. Care to join me?"

Adam didn't hesitate. He nodded.

In a few minutes, they left the yard through a gate in the back fence and followed a path through the grass to the woods. Since the path was narrow, he fell into place behind her. The trail ambled through the trees, then followed a tiny creek, still flowing from the spring rains, upward into national forest land.

His eyes were drawn to her slender but shapely form as she jogged in front of him. Her legs were smooth as silk and lightly tanned up to the point where her jogging shorts fluttered against her thighs, exposing paler flesh above the material. He was seized with a desire to see her all over, in bright daylight, to explore to his heart's content, to build the passion one caress at a time until she wrapped those perfect legs around him...

He breathed in shallow drafts as his body reacted to his thoughts. "I'm going to do some sprints," he told her, coming up beside her at a slightly wider place.

She nodded.

Pouring on the speed, he pounded down the trail, pushing himself to a breakneck pace until his breathing deepened and all his energy was focused on the bene-fits of a good, long workout. When he at last turned back and joined her for the final leg of her run, he was in con-trol once more.

At the house, they startled the doe and her babies as they munched on roses through the fence. Roni laughed when the three dashed off into the woods, tails high.

Adam followed her across the lawn, which had been mysteriously mowed in their absence. "Do you have a band of brownies who do the lawn while you're out?"

He held the back screen door open for her to precede him into the cottage.

"Even better," she told him, "a teenage neighbor who always needs money for his car."

As she passed him, the tantalizing scent of her co-logne and shampoo, the pure womanly essence of her that he'd come to know that night at the ranch, filled his nostrils. Hunger and longing washed over him like a sudden, warm rain.

As if sensing the rise of passion in him, she stopped abruptly in the doorway and looked up. Her eyes, those incredible Dalton blue eyes, widened, then darkened as an answering hunger awoke in her.

Locking her gaze with his, she laid a hand on his perspiration-soaked T-shirt as if testing the beat of his heart and the strength of his desire.

He should remove her hand. He should walk away. He should go to his room and close the door. Yeah, he knew all the things he should do, but they didn't jibe with those that he *wanted* to do.

When he stepped forward, she did, too. He let the screen door close behind them. He stood there as if suspended in time by some gleeful wizard intent on torturing him with the nearness, the promise of her.

Without conscious direction, he bent his head. She tilted hers back. He wanted the kiss so much he could taste it—the softness of her lips, the sweetness of her mouth, the response of her passion to his.

He tried to think of something, anything! "How about a milk shake?" he asked, his voice hoarse with the effort of speaking. "I know where they serve the best chocolate shake in town."

She blinked and dropped her hand, then nodded. He tried not to see the disappointment in her eyes.

"Twenty minutes," he told her huskily. "You can have the shower first."

She dashed for the bathroom as if afraid he would change his mind. In less than a minute the shower came on.

At once images came to him of them in there together. He imagined soaping his hands and running them all over her shapely figure. He exhaled loudly. It would take a lot longer than five minutes for them to shower if he joined her.

What made the hunger worse was the knowledge that she would welcome him. At least, he was pretty sure she would. She didn't do a lot to hide her interest in sharing more than the cottage with him.

They'd worked well together that morning. Was this the way marriage could be?

After drinking down a cool glass of water, he went to his room. In a few minutes he heard her call out, "All clear." He got a glimpse of wet hair and a towel-wrapped body before she closed the door to the other bedroom. He decided he needed a cool shower. A cold one, he amended when he entered the bathroom and smelled her cologne.

Ten minutes later, he joined her in the living room, showered and shaved and under control once more.

"Does this place have banana splits?" she asked when he picked up his car keys from the bowl on the coffee table where he'd started depositing them when he came home…to the cottage, he corrected. It wasn't his home.

"The best," he assured her.

"That's what I want. I'll share it with you if you'll share the milk shake with me."

"Deal." He escorted her to his car, saw her in and started off.

"You'd better be careful," she warned in cheerful

tones that belied the words, "I might construe this invitation as a date."

"Maybe it is one," he heard himself reply in the same tone. He frowned at the implied intimacy.

She patted his arm gently. "Don't analyze it to death. Let's just be a couple who are having an enjoyable day to themselves."

He nodded. He could handle that. Waving to her neighbors, who were once again tending their flowers, he wondered if they'd had an enjoyable nap

"What are you smiling about?" Roni demanded.

"Fred and Ethel," he said with partial candor.

"I imagine they got teased a lot when *I Love Lucy* first started on television."

"I'm sure they did. I once worked with an agent named Howard Hughes. People were always asking him if he had any spare money he wanted to get rid of."

As they laughed and chatted on the short trip to the ice cream shop, he realized he liked her laughter and the clean floral fragrance that surrounded her. He liked the openness of her expression and the warmth in her eyes, her apparent rapport with the elderly couple. A man could grow used to being with a woman like her...

But then in six months, he'd have to get used to the loneliness again. He forced the soaring ideas back to terra firma. He'd been through his father's death, his mother's, then the worry of his kid sister getting hurt because of him. He knew instinctively that he'd never get over it if Roni was killed because she'd had the misfortune to be married to him…

No way, he reminded that part of himself that kept thinking this marriage thing might work. He knew better, but Roni, with her bright optimism, somehow made him want to believe in forever all over again.

Chapter Ten

Roni stood in front of the closet. Time was running out, and she hadn't decided on an outfit for the dinner that night. Hearing Adam come out of his bedroom, she opened her door a crack and peeked into the living room.

He was standing at a window, his eyes on the western sky, his tall muscular body clad in a dark suit with a white shirt and somber tie. He had a commanding presence, this man she'd married, this husband of one week.

Whether he had chosen her willingly or not, he was the one who'd demanded marriage. It was time, in her opinion, that it became real, even if it was for only six months.

Tossing off her robe, she donned black undies, then pulled on black thigh-high stockings. She was reaching for a black pantsuit with wide legs of chiffon that made it look like a skirt and a long-sleeved chiffon top, both lined with black satiny material except for the sleeves, when her name was called.

"Yes? In here," she responded.

"Look out the window. There's a new family of deer in the back," Adam said in a soft voice, pushing open the door that she'd left ajar and entering the room.

They froze at the same instant.

His eyes roamed over her, lighting fires wherever they paused. His hands clenched into fists. She took a deep breath, then crossed to the window and surveyed the yard.

He'd seen her naked, so why the nervousness at him seeing her in underclothes? After all, they were married. She tried to act normal. Whatever that was.

"Yes, I see them," she told him, whispering because the window was open and she didn't want to frighten the young doe and her spotted fawn. She smiled over her shoulder. "They're eating my favorite roses."

He joined her at the window, causing a wave of heat to rush along her right side. They observed the deer as the little family moseyed along the back of the lawn.

When Adam touched her shoulder, a tremor joined the heat. She resisted an urge to lean against him.

"Easy," he murmured, running a finger along her back. "The bruises are clearing up. They're mostly yellow with a tinge of green in the center."

He stopped at her bra strap, then followed its line down her back. Her nipples peaked in wanton display, but there was nothing she could do to stop it. When both his hands settled at her waist, she stopped resisting and stepped back one step. He steppèd forward.

Against her hip, she felt the evidence of his desire. Moving instinctively, she demanded more, wanting him with every particle of her being.

With a muffled curse, he spun and left the room. "We need to leave in ten minutes," he said and closed the door without looking her way.

She stood there a second, feeling bereft and not sure what she'd done to cause this strange rift. The afternoon had gone quite well, she thought. True, Adam had withdrawn somewhat after their treat at the ice cream store, but his eyes, ah, a wealth of tenderness had flickered in those fathomless depths at times. She wondered if he knew.

But then, with the return to the house, he'd become distant again. She didn't understand him. She wished she could talk to someone—Uncle Nick or maybe Seth, but for reasons known only to her innermost heart, she couldn't.

An odd loneliness filled her. She remembered experiencing the same emotion when she'd realized her father was never coming back, when Aunt Milly and Tink had disappeared, when her brothers had gone off to college and she was left behind. She didn't have much staying power if she was discouraged after only a week. But Adam was remote, and she...she was lonely.

Determined to be cheerful at all costs, she dressed in the black outfit, slipped on the black high-heeled sandals, checked her hair and makeup, then lifted her chin and went out to face Adam.

He looked her over as if she were a mannequin on display. "Very nice." He opened the door and waited for her to precede him to his car. He was silent on the trip.

"Does Geena know we're married?" she asked.

"Yes. She saw the announcement in the paper."

In a few minutes, they pulled into the parking lot at the telecommunications company. Adam knew exactly where to go. They entered a side door that was unlocked, then an elevator, which required a code before it glided smoothly to the highest floor of the building.

Muted sounds of voices and laughter greeted them. They went into the executive lounge, strikingly decorated in tan and black with splashes of antique gold and deep aquamarine blue in the accessories.

"Hello," Geena called and came forward to exchange hugs and kisses.

Roni didn't know how that social custom got started, but she thought it was definitely time to end it as the tall blonde turned from her to Adam, her embrace much warmer and more than a tad too long, in Roni's opinion.

So who asked you? some hateful part of herself asked.

Geena made sure they had drinks, then introduced them to various company directors and officers before stopping beside her father and Scott.

"I understand congratulations are in order," the older man said jovially. "I wish you every happiness." His handshake was firm and cordial. "Danielle couldn't attend tonight, but she said to give you this." He handed an envelope to Roni.

Surprised, she opened it and found a generous gift certificate from an expensive home products store. "Thank you," she said to Charles. "This is more than kind. Please convey my appreciation…our appreciation to Danielle," she amended, remembering to include Adam.

After chatting a few more minutes, Mr. Masterson excused himself to greet another guest. Greg Williams, the financial officer, said hello then engaged Adam in a private conversation about the leasing agreement they were working on. Scott studied her for a minute.

"That was sudden," he finally said.

There was a petulance in him that she didn't find attractive. "Not really," she said coolly. "Adam and I have known for a year that there was an attraction. With the family connection, we weren't sure we should act on it."

"But then you did."

"Yes." She sipped the cool white wine and glanced around the opulent lounge. Original art hung from a picture rail around the walls. Vases were filled with sprays of spring flowers.

"I heard you leave your room that weekend at our place. You went to his. Did you sleep together there?"

"No!" She was shocked that Scott would bring the subject up, that he'd known she'd gone to Adam, albeit for the most innocent of reasons.

He looked skeptical and angry.

She lifted her chin. "We didn't decide it was real between us until the following weekend. We drove up to the ranch together for a birthday dinner for us and my uncle."

"And that's when you realized you were mad about each other?"

She laughed. "Sort of. When I was thrown from a horse, Adam was very concerned and…caring." She let the one word carry a wealth of meaning. "We decided we couldn't live without each other," she ended with a smile. Spotting Geena hanging on to Adam's arm, she murmured, "Excuse me," and left Scott to his unwarranted jealousy.

Going to her husband's right side, she leaned into him just a tiny bit, feeling her jealousy was justified. Geena still wanted Adam and didn't try to hide her interest.

When Adam put an arm around her and rested his hand on her shoulder, she suppressed an impulse to rub her cheek against his knuckles. She needed his touch and the warmth that enclosed her in his presence.

Glancing at his handsome face with its strong angles and planes, she noticed how attentively he listened to Geena as she competently discussed the leasing program with him and Greg. He'd said he would choose Geena if he were going to get involved with a woman, but would he have married her?

The idea was so painful, Roni had to stare at a painting entitled *The Dawn of Time* until she was calm once more.

"What do you think?" Adam asked, seeing her interest. He drew her aside from the other two and they studied the painting together.

"Well, it sort of looks like a big black mosquito sitting on a boulder of blue granite with the sun coming up behind it," she said honestly.

He nodded. "Mosquitoes have probably been around since the beginning." His grin was conspiratorial.

"That's by one of the foremost artists in New York," Geena noted, joining them. She held her glass out to Adam. "Darling, would you get me another glass of wine?"

"Sure. How about you?" he asked Roni.

She shook her head. "No, thanks. I get dizzy if I have more than one."

After he left them, Geena turned to Roni. "If you want to keep him, don't wear your heart on your sleeve," she advised in a kind manner. "Men, especially one like Adam, don't like to be possessed."

Roni returned the cat-in-the-cream smile. "I'll be careful. Is that what happened with your husband?"

Geena laughed. "I dumped him. A woman wants a strong man, but not an autocrat." She paused. "And a strong man needs a wife who can stand up to him."

"I thought a woman was supposed to stand *by* her man," Roni said innocently.

"True. Adam could go far with the right woman beside him." With that, Geena strolled away, looking like a princess in an ice-blue dress that went very well with the decor of the room.

Roni considered the last remark. Geena apparently didn't think a little thing like marriage could stand in the way of what she wanted. However, she knew Adam worked for the FBI. Did she think she could lure him away from his career into a position elsewhere?

"Dinner," a man in formal butler attire announced.

Roni looked around for Adam. Geena was already leading him into the dining room. Roni set her jaw. She'd always been as good at playground games as any kid on the block. Time to dust off her skills.

Falling in beside Mr. Masterson, she smiled beguilingly at him, then exclaimed softly upon entering the other room. Through floor to ceiling windows, the city was spread out before them like a gift of sparkling jewels.

"It is lovely, isn't it?" her host said.

Mr. Masterson seated her to his right and took his place at the end of the table. At the other end, Geena served as hostess in her stepmother's absence. After politely helping with her chair, Adam stood there for a second, then, like a cat scenting prey, looked her way.

At that moment, Scott slid into the chair next to her. He finished off a drink, then signaled a waiter for another.

Roni shifted uneasily, sensing hostile undercurrents from the son toward Adam. She observed the younger man as he stared at Adam with a narrowed gaze. Down the long shining table, Geena laughed at something Adam said and laid a hand on his arm.

A cold shaft of anger hit Roni. Scott and his sister had better watch their step. Adam was part of her family now and the Daltons took care of their own.

Shaking off the fury, she determined to be charming to her host, polite and distant to his son. Thus she maintained a balance throughout the toasts and congratulations on the new contract, the excellent dinner and the perfect cheesecake for dessert. They returned to the lounge for coffee. Silver servers of nuts and mints were thoughtfully placed on the low tables.

Another hour crept by. At last people started to leave. Adam came to her. "Ready to go?"

She nodded.

When Scott bid her good-night, he gallantly kissed her hand. There was hunger in his eyes when he let her go.

Roni felt a sudden pity for him. It probably stemmed from the pity she'd felt for herself off and on during the evening, she decided on the trip to the cottage. This platonic marriage business wasn't much fun, especially when another woman made her intentions clear.

"Don't lead Scott around by the nose," Adam said, breaking into her introspection. He turned into the drive and switched off the engine, then came around to open her door when she sat in the car, stunned by his words.

She got out and marched along the flagstones to the porch. "I don't intend to," she replied and went into the house, resisting a temptation to slam the door in his face. She'd done that last weekend and didn't want to be too predictable.

"Huh," was his skeptical response.

Roni turned on him. She stared, then stepped up close. "You have lipstick on you," she accused. "On your mouth."

He wiped a white handkerchief over his mouth,

glanced at the smear of color and shrugged as if it didn't matter.

"You won't find *my* lipstick on Scott," she said.

"I damned well better not!"

Roni glared while Adam threw his jacket on a chair. His tie joined it. His shoes landed beside the chair. He opened the buttons on the shirt with quick, savage motions—she was surprised that they didn't all go flying off—then went to the kitchen and poured a glass of milk. His gaze was furious and threatening as he took a long drink.

She felt the anger building inside her. She knew she should go to her room. It was late. She was tired. The air was volatile and precarious between them. She was beyond caring.

"That sword can cut both ways," she told him. "I'd better not find *her* lipstick on you ever again. I didn't ask for this marriage. That was your idea. Yours and Uncle Nick's. Well, you got it, but there are rules."

He slapped the glass on the counter. "Such as?"

"Fidelity for as long as we're legally bound. No sneak kisses between you and Geena. No clandestine meetings. No affair in any sense of the word. No…no…" Her list ran out.

"The same goes for you and Scott. And any other old lovers you might happen to run into."

"Old lovers," she repeated, scoffing at the idea. "What old lovers? You know you're the one and only."

He stepped closer and got in her face. "Now that you've had a taste, you might decide you want more."

She was astounded at the idea, then hurt, then, like a wounded creature who has to strike back, she pounced. Slamming her hands on her hips, she informed him, "Don't worry. It wasn't *that* great."

Before the words were hardly out of her mouth, she knew it was the wrong thing to say. But nothing would induce her to take them back.

"Is that right?" he asked softly.

A chill made every hair on her head stand on end. She nodded and headed for her room at a nonchalant pace.

Adam tried to hold on, to keep his cool as a red volcanic haze formed in front of his eyes and a sound like a runaway freight train roared in his ears. It was no use.

One step, one quick grab and he had her by the wrist, halting her self-righteous exit.

"Is that right?" he demanded again.

She shrugged delicately. Her pretended indifference was a challenge he couldn't ignore.

"Who moaned like a banshee when we kissed?" he asked very, very softly. "Who pressed against me and wanted more...and more...and more?"

She stared into space and said nothing.

"Who experienced pleasure so deep, so strong she came apart in my arms? Who wanted it again in less than thirty minutes?"

He saw her swallow and a blush creep up her neck and into her face. However, he had to admire her control as she merely raised her eyebrows as if to ask if he was through.

He answered the silent, haughty question by continuing his plaint. "Who then slept like a babe and didn't give a thought to anything but the passion between us, although others also slept in the house?"

Her eyes widened at that. "Who came to my room, pretending compassion while soothing my bruises?"

He nodded, accepting the barb of truth.

"Who went beyond the Good Samaritan act with his touches and caresses until I couldn't think of anything but the hunger, the *mutual* hunger, that we shared?"

Yeah, he'd done that.

"Who stayed when it was wiser to leave? Who took all the passion I could give? Who went to sleep in my bed and didn't return to his own room, even though he'd left his door open so that it was obvious to anyone who glanced in that his bed hadn't been used?"

"Touché," he said when she fell silent.

She'd hit a sore spot. He wasn't too proud of the way he'd succumbed to their hunger, knowing she wasn't experienced, knowing she was most likely confusing desire with emotion, knowing she probably believed that great passion was synonymous with great love.

"If we're going to have a platonic marriage," she said, "then it's going to be platonic for both of us. I won't put up with an affair. And don't let Geena kiss you again…unless you want the biggest scene since Mount Saint Helens blew up. I can promise that's what you'll get."

When she yanked against his hold on her wrist, he let her go. Funny feelings bumped around in his chest,

a whole grab bag of them, when she entered her bedroom and closed the door solidly behind her. After a
tense moment of indecision, he went out on the front
porch to let the night's chill cool him off while he
thought things through.

Sitting in a rickety chair, he wondered what the hell
had happened to him tonight. He'd always kept control
of any situation he was in, but now he found himself on
the verge of caveman acts.

Like beating the door down and showing her how
good it had been between them.

Like making love to her until they were too exhausted
to move and she admitted it was the best thing she'd ever
experienced.

Like holding her while she slept tucked up against
him, so contented, so deep in sleep she hadn't been
aware of the sunrise or the lateness of the hour.

But then, neither had he.

Uneasiness swirled around the void inside him. He'd
been in dangerous situations before. He'd lived through
times when he'd thought his life was going to end within
the next moment. Huh. At present he wasn't sure he
would make it through the next second, much less a
whole minute.

Six months.

He groaned and headed for his room, hating the ex-
pansiveness of the queen-size bed that offered the promise of bliss, but held only emptiness.

It was his own fault, he admitted. Unable to resist,

he'd taken advantage of her inexperience and the attraction that existed between them. He should never have gone to her room that night.

But he had, and now they were both paying the consequences.

With a sigh, he threw off his clothes and got into the empty bed. His libido at once perked up. The sheets held the scent of roses and lavender and a thousand other delicate aromas that reminded him of her. Only her.

If his stubborn little bride knew how seldom he'd thought of Geena or any other woman since the first moment he'd met her, she would laugh her head off. She was like a magic potion, bubbling through his blood, making him dream of home and happiness and a host of other things he no longer believed in, not for himself at any rate.

After a restless half hour, he retrieved the guitar from its case and strummed it softly. In the past, the music had helped lull him to sleep. As he played a ballad, an idle thought popped into his head. Maybe they should make a stab at this marriage thing. Maybe it could work—

Damn. Now he was getting as bad as his romantic-minded wife who thought all would work out if they really, really tried. Life had never been that kind, not to him.

He thought of his father, an innocent man who'd wanted only the freedom to raise his family in peace, of his sister who'd been put in danger because of his work, of Roni who filled his head with foolish wonder with her delight in flowers or a deer family, her easy friendship with her neighbors, her absolute loyalty to those she loved.

Pain flashed through him, composed of part desire, part frustration and part…something. He couldn't name the other thing, but he knew what it was, deep in his heart, he knew…

Chapter Eleven

Roni had never known time could creep by so slowly or speed by so fast, all at the same instant. At work, June had been hectic so far and they were only two weeks into the month.

Today was a crucial day for her company. If the stock offering went well, henceforth it would be known as iLearn, rather than the Boise Learning Center as in the past. Her life could change a lot, too, depending on what happened today.

Glancing at the calendar, she paused with a little start. The date was June the thirteenth. And it was Friday.

"Silly," she scolded. She didn't believe in bad luck. People brought their fates on themselves by their actions and decisions.

She fixed her usual yogurt, cereal and fruit and sat at

the island to eat. The sun was just coming up. The two does and their fawns were munching on her roses. Apparently word of her place was spreading among the deer community. She smiled as another blossom disappeared.

Behind her, a door opened. She glanced over her shoulder in time to see Adam enter the bathroom, his body lithe, muscular and sexy in white briefs. The shower came on. Five minutes later, it stopped.

She imagined him shaving, maybe muttering a low curse when he nicked himself, then putting a dab of tissue on the wound to stop the bleeding as her uncle had. She and the other kids had snickered at this home remedy. They'd preferred strips of colorful bandages, the more scrapes and cuts one could find to cover, the better.

A jab of the strange loneliness that had haunted her as of late hit her. Due to work, she hadn't been to the ranch since the wedding. Mmm, that was three weeks ago. It only seemed a lifetime. She grimaced wryly.

Adam emerged from his room wearing suit pants and a white shirt. Through the open door, she could see his dark jacket and tie on the neatly made bed.

"Good morning." He paused to look her black pantsuit over. "This is your day at the office, isn't it?"

"Yes." She just had to share her excitement with someone. Adam had avoided her since their quarrel, but he was her husband. Who was more appropriate to share the information with? "It's our *big* day. Cascade Learning Center is going public as iLearn. Jerry's in New York for the IPO."

"Initial public offering," Adam translated. "What's the opening price on the stock?"

"Ten dollars. Five million shares." She held up her right hand, fingers crossed. "Here's hoping the price goes up...or at least holds steady until the closing bell," she added, recalling the vagaries of the stock market.

Adam whistled. "A cool fifty million." He took a drink of coffee, then prepared a bowl of cereal with bananas and nectarines. After adding milk, he took the stool beside her. "Didn't you say you had a stake in the company?"

She nodded and swallowed the last bite of her meal. "I've been getting shares every year since I've been there."

He considered, then asked, "How many shares do you have now?"

"Twenty-five thousand."

She tried to act casual as she put her bowl and spoon in the dishwasher and refilled her cup. Resting both elbows on the counter across from him, she sipped the hot brew and observed the light dawn in his eyes as he realized just what that meant in dollars and cents.

"A quarter mil," he said. "At ten dollars a share, you'll be worth a quarter million."

"Maybe. I can't sell any stock for seven months, else the feds can get me for insider trading. But if the price holds up that long, I'll be rich. Almost." She couldn't contain the triumphant grin.

"How much more would it take for you to feel really wealthy," he asked, returning her smile.

"A million," she promptly answered. "I couldn't sleep last night for thinking about today."

"I heard you at your computer."

"Yes. I worked on the new game." She hesitated, then decided to confess all. "There's more. G-2, the guy I work with, and I talked Jerry into trying the computer game field a couple of years ago. Our first one went on the market recently. It sold out in a month. Last week, the company ordered another 50,000 CDs. G-2 and I will get royalties since it was our idea."

"How much?" Adam asked, wry humor in his words.

"Well," she began modestly, not wanting to brag, "it could be as much as a hundred thousand."

"Or more?"

She nodded. "You should put in an order for shares of iLearn. Seth says it's a good buy."

"How much should one invest?"

She was serious when she said, "Ten thousand dollars would be a good stake."

He raised his cup in a toast. "I'll keep it in mind."

"If you don't happen to have ten grand lying about, I'll be glad to float you a loan."

This time he chuckled at her smart-mouth remark. "Feeling your oats, aren't you?"

She laughed, hugged herself and danced around the tiny kitchen. "I'm delirious," she admitted. "I've thought of a million ways to spend the money."

"Let's go out to dinner tonight," he invited. "It isn't every day a guy finds himself married to a millionaire."

"We're not there yet," she cautioned, pleasure erupting at his grin. "But I'm hoping." She held up crossed fingers and whirled in a giddy circle.

When she lost her balance and stumbled against the stove, Adam was there to steady her before she fell. She leaned against his arm and gazed into his handsome face.

Except for the pounding of her heart, she went utterly still. Waves of intense longing washed through her, but she schooled herself to patience although she wanted his kiss more than any amount of money she could ever imagine.

Slowly he bent his head.

When he touched her mouth, she wrapped her arms around him and returned the kiss, lost in desire and need and love.

He gave a soft moan and ran his hands over her, slanting his mouth over hers in first one direction, then the other. With tongues and lips and hands, they caressed each other with a wild unappeased hunger. At last he held her off. "It's time to go," he murmured huskily.

"Yes."

"Don't forget dinner."

Her heart was singing. "It's a date."

Tonight. She couldn't think of anything else as she wove her way through the morning traffic. *Tonight.*

That afternoon Adam looked over the bank information, the transcript of the tapped telephone conversations and the intercepted e-mails. He nodded to the new agent who'd been assigned to assist him. "We have an airtight case. Get a court order and we'll close 'em down."

"Right!" the assistant agent said smartly, all but saluting. He'd recently been in military intelligence.

After the man left, Adam wondered if he'd ever been as young and idealistic as this fresh-faced kid. Once maybe, when he'd been about ten and all had been right with his world. With his parents' deaths, he'd lost faith in mankind.

Had he not had to take care of his baby sister, he wondered where he might have ended up. Prison? Dead in a gang fight? Probably.

But Honey had needed him, and he'd been determined to shield her from their aunt who hadn't wanted the extra kids, although she had wanted the money the state paid her to provide a home for them.

The ring of the telephone interrupted his ruminations. "Smith," he said into the receiver.

"Hey, Adam, Seth here. Sorry to bother you at work, but Roni's in a meeting and I didn't want to disturb her. I have a favor to ask."

"Ask away."

"I'm in town on a court case, but it looks as if it's going to carry over into a special session tomorrow. I may need a place to crash tonight. Can you and Roni put me up?"

Adam responded at once. "I'm sure we can."

Actually he wasn't sure at all. Roni wouldn't like her brother knowing things were a bit awkward at their rose-covered cottage, not while they were faking married bliss as far as her family was concerned, but hospitality was big in the Dalton family.

"Great," Seth said. "I have a meeting with my law partner when I finish at the courthouse. It'll probably be eight or nine before I get in, so tell Roni not to worry about dinner for me."

"Right. We'll look forward to seeing you."

After they hung up, Adam contemplated the evening ahead. Glancing at his watch, he decided he had better try her cell phone and let her know what was up. He got the voice mail message and left word that he was on his way home and that Seth might be spending the night.

Fifteen minutes later, he stood in the living room of the cottage and wondered where the heck they should put Seth. The sofa? Nah. The daybed in Roni's office? It was the logical place.

He hesitated, then entered her domain. The room was neat, all papers filed, computer disks stacked in special holders and pencils upright in a black and white mug shaped like a cow.

Setting his jaw, he stripped the mattress, got sheets from the linen closet in the bathroom and made it up again. Gathering the used sheets into a bundle, he took them to a tiny laundry room/pantry off the kitchen. There he started the washer and threw in a cup of detergent.

As he dropped the linens into the machine, the faint fragrance of roses wafted around him. Without thinking, he brought the pillowcase to his nose and inhaled deeply.

The rush of hunger was so powerful it made him dizzy. Blood flowed in a tidal wave from his head to his groin. He groaned and pressed his face into the material.

He realized his mistake as her scent engulfed him, filled him, saturated him with need and longing of a kind he'd never experienced.

"What is this?" he muttered as pain followed the hunger. "What the hell is this?"

As if it were a burning object, he dropped the pillow-case into the steaming water, banged the lid closed and headed to his room. After changing into jogging shorts, T-shirt and shoes, he set out along the path through the woods. A good fast run, and a long one, was all he needed to clear his head.

An hour later he returned to the house, dripping sweat after pushing himself harder than he'd ever done. Roni was on the phone when he entered the back door.

She smiled at him while continuing her conversation. Her bare feet were propped on the stool where he usually sat. A long stretch of smooth shapely leg led his eye upward to jogging shorts that had an inch-long slit up the side. A wisp of pink lace was visible there.

The exhaustion of the hard run fled his body. Energy as fresh as morning dew, as strong as a mountain storm, licked through his veins. He froze in place, unable to move or take his eyes from her, his beautiful, tempting wife.

She hung up the phone and turned to him with a glow. "That was my boss. The stock closed three dollars above the opening price with a steady gain throughout the day. The brokerage company was pleased. We're off to a good start."

Her smile was so brilliant, it filled him with light. "Great. Where shall we go to celebrate?"

"How about here? I don't think I can face the Friday night traffic again." At his nod, she continued, "I got your message about Seth. He called. He says he'll be in around ten, the way things are looking."

Adam nodded. "I, uh, made up the bed in your room."

"Ah, that explains the sheets in the washer when I arrived. They're dry now. I put them away when I saw the clean sheets on the bed. Are you sleeping with me?"

She tilted her head and studied him as she waited for an answer. Her gaze was lambent, an invitation in the deep blue depths. He had only to reach out...

"I thought, after Seth went to bed, I would sleep on the sofa. You can have your old room to yourself."

The brilliance dimmed. "That won't work. Seth will report to Uncle Nick if all isn't well here."

Adam heaved an exasperated breath. Deal with one Dalton and you dealt with all of them. "I can suddenly be called out," he said, trying to come up with an explanation for his absence. "I'll get a motel—"

"They're full," Roni informed him. "There's a software convention in town today, tomorrow and Sunday. Haven't you been keeping up with the news?"

"So what would you suggest?" he asked, his voice tight as frustration broke through.

She shrugged and crossed one leg over the other,

swinging the upper one with studied nonchalance. "We've shared a bed before."

He shook his head. Since the marriage, he'd tried to keep complications between them to a minimum. The kiss this morning had been ill-advised. No way could he share a bed with her and guarantee celibacy.

So why not take what they both wanted?

He ignored the insidious urging inside his head and voiced a wiser idea. "A clean divorce with no complications is the right way to go."

She blinked as if he'd struck her. "We certainly wouldn't want to complicate things, now would we?" She hopped off the stool, pulled on socks and running shoes and headed out the back door.

Going to the door, he thought of telling her exercise wouldn't cure what ailed them. He'd just spent a futile hour on the jogging trail, trying to quell his physical need while denying there were any other aspects to their relationship. The latter he knew was a lie. Things were getting serious. He needed to leave.

Tomorrow he and four other agents would raid Greg's office and confiscate the files. With the information he and his assistant had collected on the con artist, the case was all but finished. Then what?

A new assignment. Maybe the one in New Mexico was still open. He and Roni would have their excuse for the divorce and could call it quits.

Or they could live happily ever after, some sly part of him suggested.

The battle between his conscience and the ever-present need for her had waged through him all day. As he observed her lithe form until she disappeared along the wooded path, he considered following her just to be sure she was safe, then realized he was probably the biggest danger to her in his present state. He wearily headed to the bathroom for a long, chilling shower.

When his wife returned, he put two chicken breasts on the grill to cook. After bathing and dressing in a blue fleecy outfit, she made salads and zapped corn on the cob in the microwave. They ate in total silence.

Later, each of them worked at their computers, her in the office/guest room, him on his laptop at the kitchen counter. Seth arrived at five minutes before ten, briefcase and a plastic bag from the local mall in hand. Adam opened the front door and invited him inside.

"Man, I'm beat," his new brother-in-law told them, crossing the room to kiss Roni on the forehead. "The store was crowded when I stopped to get some clean clothes."

"You can wash your things here," Roni said, her manner sympathetic.

"Too much trouble. And I'm too lazy," he added with a candid grimace. "Mind if I take a quick shower?"

"Of course not. You know where the towels are."

For a second, Adam found himself envying the other man's ease with Roni. Although they had only that winter discovered that Seth wasn't truly her half-brother, the family bond had existed since Roni was barely more than a toddler. Her loyalty to Seth ran as deep as any blood tie.

As it would with her husband.

He set his teeth while the familiar whirl of emotions sucked him into its black center. He'd learned long ago to hold on, to simply survive from one minute to the next until the pain went away. He stared mindlessly at the weather news on the television screen until the moment passed.

When Seth rejoined them, Roni spooned up bowls of nonfat frozen yogurt and topped them with strawberries.

"Man, that was good," her brother said when his bowl was empty. He covered a yawn. "Sorry, but I'm off to bed. I was up with the birds this morning."

Roni wasn't at all sympathetic. "You knew before you married her that Amelia wakes up early. When dawn breaks, she thinks she should be there to sweep up the pieces."

Seth laughed uproariously at the quip and said he had to remember it to tell his wife.

Adam helped Roni put the used dishes in the dishwasher. "That could apply to you, too," he said, keeping his voice low. "You get up with the sun."

"Does it bother you?" she asked with a somberness that was new to their relationship. "I try to be quiet."

"No. I like the morning, too."

She nodded. It did something to him to know she cared enough to be concerned. A man could get used to that—

He broke the thought and headed for the door. "I think I'll get some air before heading to bed."

Outside, the mountain air cooled his blood. When he was sure he was in total control once more, he went inside, locked the front and back doors, then entered the bedroom, quietly closing that door behind him.

His breath froze in his throat. He leaned against the wall as his legs went weak. Roni stood in front of the dresser, brushing her hair. A negligee was tossed over a chair. She wore the matching gown of pink satin with lace inserts at the sides and over her breasts.

Their gazes met in the mirror and locked. She turned to him, an invitation of earthly delights.

"What the hell are you trying to do to me?" he demanded in a hoarse voice.

"Be your wife?" she suggested softly.

There was only one defense he could think of. "I thought I told you—a wife is something I've never wanted."

He was able—barely—to summon the energy and the willpower to force his body from the room and pretend he didn't see the way she went pale, her fair skin seeming to change to marble before his eyes.

Roni waved Seth off, then closed the door against the morning chill. The house was eerily quiet. Adam, like a night fog that couldn't survive in sunlight, had disappeared with the dawn. She didn't know where he'd slept or if he had after he'd walked out of the bedroom. She'd had the queen-size bed to herself.

A sense of failure settled over her spirits. Her elation of the previous day had evaporated in the cold face of reality. Even the most ardent of wild-eyed optimists reached a point where they had to give up. Trying really, really hard did not ensure success. As her attempt at seduction last night had clearly proved.

A wife is something I've never wanted.

Adam had been honest about that from the beginning, so she couldn't say she hadn't known. Naturally, with the marriage, she'd hoped, but...

"Ah, well," she murmured. Life was just one learning experience after another.

After stripping all the sheets, she tossed them in the washer, then cleaned the cottage, a task she hadn't done thoroughly since the wedding. When the whole place was neat and shining, she checked supplies and went to the grocery.

At home once more, she stored the boxes and cans, then slathered apple slices with peanut butter and ate them along with nonfat milk for lunch. She worked on the quilt for twenty minutes, then, too restless to sit, went for a short jog and a long walk.

Her family was big on planning, but for the life of her she couldn't think what to do next.

When she returned to the house, the telephone was ringing. The machine picked it up before she could. She listened as the caller left a message, then hung up.

Going into the bathroom, she showered, considered the options and realized there were none.

Adam and his partner, plus four other agents, walked into the headquarters building of CTC. They'd chosen to act on Saturday since the building would be mostly empty.

Geena met them in the lobby. "He's here."

"Good." Adam held up the warrant. "We'll have to take his records, computers, everything."

She grimaced. "I know. My father is in his office. Is it okay if I tell him what's happening?"

"Yes. This way," he said to the men.

Greg Williams looked up in annoyance when the six agents walked into his office without knocking. "What the hell?" he said, then recognized Adam. "What are you doing here? I said I'd see you next week."

Adam flashed his badge. "I'm a little early," he said.

Greg sprang to his feet as if he would run, but the phalanx in front of him proved too discouraging. He stayed where he was, his face contorted in fury.

"You're under arrest. You have the right to remain silent," Adam intoned and cited the rest of the rights.

While he cuffed Greg, the other agents began to box the computer equipment and pack files into the boxes they'd brought.

"You bastard," the con man said bitterly. "You set me up. Entrapment doesn't go over with a jury."

"Hey, you cut me out," Adam reminded him. "You set up your own offshore accounts to the tune of a half million dollars of CTC's money. You did the same at the last company you worked for, the one you bankrupted while paying yourself a handsome salary, a hefty bonus and the money from deals you cut for your phony companies."

"You want me to take him in and book him?" the new agent asked, eager to be in on the kill.

Adam nodded. "Get everything, including the secret documents under the fake palm."

"How did you find out about that?" Greg demanded.

"I told him," Geena said, meeting them at the door, her father behind her. They both looked at their former financial officer with contempt.

He returned the glare, then switched to Adam. "How's the pretty little wife?" he asked with a sneer. "Checked on her lately?"

Adam narrowed his eyes, but didn't answer.

"You think I work alone?" He laughed as if he'd told a really funny joke. "I've left orders. If something happens to me, my friends will tidy up the loose ends."

The other agents paused and looked at him.

Adam felt the pain run deep at the thought of Roni being hurt. "Take him away," he told his partner. He gestured to another man. "Go with them."

The two agents left with the crook. Adam quelled an impulse to rush home as fast as he could. Even if Greg did have partners, which Adam didn't believe, the FBI had moved so fast, it would be hours before they knew what was up.

"I'll make a full report next week," he said to Mr. Masterson. "I've blocked the money transfer. The funds will be held until a court order is received to deposit them back in the company account."

"Thank God," the older man said. "Will we get the files back?"

Adam assured him they would. "And the computer and disks when we're sure we've got everything we need."

The father and daughter team stayed until the agents finished packing. Mr. Masterson left for an afternoon golf game when Adam assured him there was nothing more to do that day.

After the other agents left, Adam signed over a receipt to the daughter for everything they'd confiscated, then checked his watch.

"It's nearly one. Shall we go to the country club for lunch?" Geena asked. "I've reserved a table."

"I have to get home," he said.

"Worried about your wife?" Her tone was sardonic. "You surely don't think Greg would admit it if he really had arranged for something to happen to her."

Adam looked at the other woman and felt nothing. Not for her, at any rate. "Yes, I'm worried about my wife. I think Williams was blowing smoke, but it isn't something I can ignore."

She gestured to the telephone. "So call her."

He punched in the number of the cottage. "No answer," he said when the answering machine came on after two rings, which meant there was already a message on it. She probably wasn't at the house. However, he tried twice more in order to give Roni time to get to the phone in case she was busy.

His heart started a low, throbbing beat like a bass

drum when there was still no answer. He headed for the door.

Behind him, he heard Geena call his name, but he didn't glance back. Once in his car, he drove to the freeway and floored the accelerator, grateful the traffic was light that afternoon. He tried their home number two more times on his cell phone, then called her cell number. He attempted to leave a message but got a low battery signal before his phone went dead. He tossed it in the passenger seat in disgust. He'd forgotten to charge it last night.

That was because he'd slept at the office. After picking up his suits and shirts at the cleaners and buying a new tie, he'd also showered and dressed there before the other agents arrived for the big bust.

At the cottage, he knew the house was empty as soon as he arrived. Her car wasn't in the drive and the front door was locked. Maybe she'd gone to the grocery. He went inside.

Seeing the message indicator on the phone, he hit the button and listened.

Roni, this is Geena. Adam is here at CTC with some other agents. They're in the process of arresting Greg Williams. This wraps up the case, except for the trial. Adam has been absolutely brilliant, but of course you know that. I've reserved a table at the country club to celebrate. Come join us if you like.

Geena's satisfied laughter floated into the room, then stopped abruptly when she hung up.

"Damn," Adam muttered.

A beep signaled the end of one message and the beginning of another.

"Uh, hello? Adam, this is Don Talbot. Sorry I wasn't in to catch your call this morning. The case is still open and the field manager says to get here ASAP. I look forward to working with you again. It'll be like old times, except it's hotter than hell along the border here in New Mexico."

Adam clenched his fists as understanding dawned. Roni knew he'd wrapped up one case and had inquired about another one that was out of state, far from the cozy cottage.

And from her.

With the precise logic of her sharp mind, she would link his words of last night with the two calls and come up with the right answer—that he was already making plans to leave. After seeing her in his bedroom, he'd known he had to go, or else he would be tempted to stay forever.

A wife is something I've never wanted.

"Good God," he muttered, hearing the cruelty of it as the words replayed in his head. With a certainty he didn't question, he knew where she was. Checking her room confirmed his hunch. Her weekend case was missing.

She'd go to the ranch to think things over. And to avoid him. He didn't blame her, but he had to see her and explain things, why it was better that he leave now before the situation between them exploded out of control, the way it had that night at the ranch after her fall.

In his room, he changed from his suit to more casual clothes, then packed a bag and grabbed the battery charger for the cell phone. He called his partner, told him where he was going and asked him to hold the fort until he got back.

"No problem, Adam," the younger agent said earnestly. "Don't worry about a thing."

"I know I can depend on you," Adam said and meant it. The kid had the makings of an excellent agent, and he knew computers nearly as well as Roni.

With fatalistic humor at the thought of those two talking shop if they ever met, he locked up and drove off, heading north to see for himself that she was safe and to explain that he'd never meant to hurt her.

The brief amusement disappeared, replaced by the worry he couldn't quite eradicate. If Greg hadn't been lying, then he should let Roni know so she could alert Zack and the twins to look out for strangers.

He plugged his cell phone into the car outlet, but got no answer on her phone. A computer-generated voice told him the number didn't answer. He hung up and headed toward the dark clouds on the horizon, a prayer repeating over and over in his heart as he remembered waiting for the hit men who were after his sister last year while hoping he was at the right place at the right time.

Chapter Twelve

Roni sat on the floor behind the bed, her back against the wall. Long ago, when she got into trouble—about once a week on average—she used to hide under the bed to escape the scolding she knew she'd get from her uncle or her brothers.

When she'd been eight, she'd taken her new kitten outside and let it out of its box. She'd left it while she went into the house to get a snack. The kitten had decided to nap under the station wagon. Naturally the worst had happened when one of the boys had to go to town for some horse medicine. She'd stayed under the bed all night.

That had been the start of an unspoken rule in the Dalton household. When a person needed to be alone, that need was respected.

Uncle Nick had later bought name magnets for each of them and placed them on the side of the refrigerator. If a person was going off and would be gone overnight, he or she moved their name out of the neat row and placed it in the corner so the others wouldn't worry about them.

So here she was again. History repeating itself. She was too big to hide under the bed, but she'd returned here all the same. The ranch was her sanctuary.

A sigh escaped her. She'd been wrong about her and Adam, she admitted. Love wasn't involved, nor the inevitable result of an overwhelming passion.

But last Thanksgiving, when Adam had spent a week at the ranch, he'd started calling her "Little Bits" once in a while. Since the only other person she'd heard him use a pet name with had been his sister and Roni knew Honey was the one person he loved unconditionally, she'd thought...

So she'd leaped to the wrong conclusion. Her two plus two didn't add up to love, marriage and happiness forever.

She picked up the doll from the little stroller and studied its painted face. The unblinking stare and set smile had comforted her during those long-ago days when she'd realized her father was never coming home.

The doll didn't console her now, though. She'd outgrown it, she realized with sad but tender nostalgia. "It isn't your fault," she whispered. "You haven't changed, but I have. A person has no choice."

Gently she replaced it in the stroller, then went outside to join her uncle on the porch.

The late afternoon sun wasn't visible behind the dark gathering of clouds over the surrounding peaks. Lightning flashed, but the thunder was too far away to be heard.

"The land never fails to fill me with awe," the family patriarch told her, his eyes on the mountains. "Even when it's at its most dangerous."

"I love it, too," Roni agreed, sitting in a rocker beside his chair. "It's always here, steady and unchanging in the human scheme of things. That's comforting."

"Your Aunt Milly felt that way, too," the older man said. "She insisted on exploring every part of the ranch when we first married. You and Tink loved picnics by the creek or at the Devil's Dining Room."

"I remember."

She and her uncle talked of days gone by, dwelling only on the funny things that had happened to them as a family. It was as if he knew she needed the assurance of happy memories to get her past this moment.

He didn't ask if anything was wrong, and she didn't volunteer the information. How did one announce that a marriage of less than a month was over?

"I may go up to the snow cabin for a couple of days," she finally said during a quiet spell while they watched the storm darken the sky to charcoal.

"Take a horse. The roads won't be passable if this storm brings a lot of rain." He hesitated. "You and Adam haven't worked things out yet?"

She stood. "Actually, we have." She tried a smile and

found she could hold it. "We've decided on divorce. We were going to wait six months so we could say we tried, but he's finished his work, so he'll be leaving. Seth can start the divorce proceedings right away."

On legs that felt as stable as willow twigs, she stood and kissed his cheek, then returned to her room and closed the door. She sat on the bed and covered her eyes. That way, she held the tears in.

At last finding the quiet center of herself—maybe frozen center was a better description—she gazed around the familiar room as if telling it goodbye. Slowly she rose and left the room of her childhood.

After placing her name tag up on the corner of the refrigerator, she left the house with an old backpack from high school days, going quietly outside into the warm summer light. No one was in the yard or stable when she saddled up and rode out.

The storm was close when Adam pulled to a stop in front of the horse rail at the ranch house, but no rain had fallen yet. He grabbed his bag and dashed into the house, his heart louder than the thunder that rumbled over the nearby peak.

Inside, he found Roni's uncle lighting the logs in the fireplace. There was no sign of his wife. Fear hit him in a surprise attack. "Is…" He had to clear his throat. "Is Roni here?"

Her uncle gazed at him, then said, "She isn't at the house." His tone indicated he knew where she was.

"Where is she? In town? At the B and B?" Adam asked when the older man fell silent.

"She's safe," he finally said. "Let's make some coffee, then we'll talk."

Adam set his case down and went into the kitchen. He knew there was no use in arguing that he needed to see his wife right away. Uncle and niece were a stubborn lot. The patriarch would tell him where Roni was when he was ready and not a second before.

Uncle Nick put the coffee on, then sat at the table. Adam took a chair, suppressing the impatience that made him want to curse and shake the other man.

The old man studied him for a minute, his blue eyes, so like Roni's, gazing at him with something like sorrow in their depths. Adam stirred uneasily. When the coffee was ready, he poured two cups and returned to the table.

"The problem with old people," the uncle finally began, "is that we think we know best. Because of our long years, we think we've seen it all and can tell you young ones what you should do." He heaved a sigh.

He held up a hand when Adam started to speak.

"I thought I knew how it was for you and my niece and that marriage would fix everything," he continued.

Adam nodded. He really wasn't interested in a confession, but the old man seemed determined.

"I was wrong." Her uncle frowned. "Seth thought you two looked like hell when he spent the night at your place. He was right. It's obvious you're both miserable."

"So you've seen her? She's been here?"

"Yes. It was a mistake to force the marriage—"

"What's done is done," Adam interrupted. "Roni and I are adults. We decided our own fate."

"You told me not to push it, that neither of you were ready for that kind of commitment. I was the one who demanded you do the honorable thing by her. I should have listened. I'm sorry for interfering."

Adam waved the apology aside. He had to see Roni. Now. "Where is she? I need to talk to her."

"She wants to be alone for a while. When she's ready, she'll come back."

"Dammit," Adam said, "she's my wife. I have a right to know where she is."

"In time," Nick promised. "In time. You'll have to wait."

And nothing Adam said could change his mind.

Trevor and his twin took their cue from their uncle. They just shrugged when he spotted them at the stable and went to ask them about their cousin. "Haven't seen her," Trevor said. Travis nodded in agreement.

Adam swept the pastures with a practiced eye. His years of FBI work had taught him to catch the unusual detail, the one item that was out of place. "The mare she rides," he said. "It isn't with the others in the pasture."

Trevor peered out. "Adam's right. The mare's gone. You didn't move her, did you, bro?"

"Not since we weaned her colt," Travis said.

"Where would she go?" Adam asked.

Silence greeted the question. Trevor glanced at Adam. "*Why* did she go?"

Adam met his eyes. Dalton eyes. Roni's eyes. He didn't want to think about his wife's state of mind. Fear gnawed at him even as he assured himself that Roni wouldn't do anything stupid. She was too smart, too independent, for that.

But he'd seen her eyes when she'd stood in the bedroom in the pretty pink gown she'd worn for him. There had been darkness in those blue depths, a haunting despair that could overwhelm a person. He knew. It matched the darkness in himself.

"Let's save the postmortem for after we find her," he said and wondered where to look for clues to his elusive mate's whereabouts. Since her family wasn't going to help, he would do it himself.

Roni cut some brush with a hatchet from the line cabin and patched the holes in the rickety corral before turning the mare loose in it. She carried her tack into the cabin and laid it in a corner, then set about gathering wood for the old Franklin stove. She would need a fire for heating the canned soup as well as for warmth. The storm blowing in off the mountains brought a chill with it.

After filling the wood box, she sat on the flat stone that served as a stoop and gazed at the distant peaks. The last visible traces of snow were gone, although some might linger in cool, protected pockets under the trees.

Well, it was almost midyear. The days were getting warmer, and the snow would melt away.

Six weeks ago she'd fallen, literally, into Adam's life. Three weeks ago, they'd said their vows. Odd to think that the marriage was over after such a short time. Not that she'd started out with terribly high hopes, but this wasn't the way things were supposed to be.

At the moment, she couldn't, for the life of her, figure out why she'd thought they would live the sappy storybook ending. What a dreamer!

The mare lifted her nose into the breeze and sniffed delicately, then shook her head and whinnied.

Roni went to the corral. "What is it, girl?"

The mare came close and thrust her nose into Roni's hand. Roni patted the animal and scratched her ears.

"We should go home," she said.

She knew she wasn't ready, not yet. She had to be certain she could maintain that calm center before she faced her family, then Adam. She had to convince herself the divorce wouldn't hurt. She wondered if he'd realized she was gone. Maybe he and Geena had extended their luncheon into dinner...

"I did love him," she murmured. "From the first moment I saw him. I wonder why."

The mare gazed at her with soft, sorrowful eyes.

"I'll get over it," Roni whispered. "You can do anything if you make up your mind to it."

She pressed her forehead against the mare's neck and waited until the hot tightness eased from her chest before going inside to start the fire.

* * *

"It's getting dark," Adam said. He stood at the door to the barn. Inside, Trevor and Travis took care of several orphaned animals, feeding them from buckets with rubber nipples attached near the bottom.

"Here," Travis thrust a bucket into his hand and pointed toward a stall.

The calf bawled indignantly at him and poked its head between the slats.

He brought the nipple to the hungry mouth and felt the strong tug on the bucket as the calf latched on. He thought of Roni nursing a child and wondered if it hurt...

Guilt pulled at him. *He* had hurt her.

When she'd walked down the aisle in her wedding finery, when her eyes had met his, when the smile had bloomed over her whole face, he'd had a glimpse of paradise.

However, he knew how brief heaven could be. He hadn't wanted to be the one to disillusion Roni. He hadn't wanted anyone's happiness depending on him.

With a silent curse, he tilted the bucket so the calf could get the last sips, then exchanged it for the full one Roni's cousin had prepared by stirring powdered formula into water. He went to the next hungry mouth in line.

"Has she stayed out overnight before?" he asked.

"Lots of times," Trevor assured him.

Adam thought of knocking the casual expression off the younger man's face. "Where does she go?"

He saw the twins exchange glances. They both shrugged.

"You know," Adam accused. "You know where she is."

A red haze gathered at the periphery of his vision. He wanted a fight. He wanted to beat something senseless until the anger and frustration were gone and he could think clearly once more. He grabbed a handful of shirt.

"Tell me," he demanded of Trevor.

"Why?"

"Why? Because, dammit, she's my wife."

Trevor yanked his shirt away. "Not good enough," he said coolly and walked out of the barn.

Adam glared at Travis. The twin gave him a level glance and continued with the chores.

"This is wilderness," he said in a reasonable voice. "She could get lost or in trouble. A bear or wildcat—"

Travis, smiling, shook his head.

Adam shut up. When the calf finished, he set the bucket on a bail of hay and stalked outside. A break in the clouds allowed a sliver of sunset to come through. It backlighted the peaks in auras of pink and gold. He wondered if Roni was looking at the twilight before he went into the house.

"Supper in ten minutes," the older man said.

Adam went to the bathroom and washed up. Unable to stop himself, he went into the rose bedroom. It reminded him of Roni—feminine in appearance yet built on a solid foundation of integrity and loyalty. She had a right to expect the same from her mate.

A giant fist grabbed his chest, squeezing until he couldn't breathe, couldn't think. He wasn't sure he would live through the night.

* * *

Roni spread a couple of blankets over the cot. The cabin had originally been built as a line shack for the ranch hands to use during roundups or fence repairs when they were in the area. Nowadays it was kept in good order mainly as a shelter during storms.

At various times, one or another of the Daltons had used it as a place of personal refuge. However, the cabin didn't seem much of a retreat anymore. Like the doll, maybe she'd outgrown it, too.

You can run, her conscience chided.

Okay, so she was hiding. She had to face Adam sooner or later. Tomorrow, she decided. When she was braver.

Hearing the mare whicker, Roni removed a flashlight from a shelf on the back wall, flicked it on and went outside. A black shape sniffed along the corral.

"Haiii," she yelled.

The bear was small, no more than a two-year-old, and most likely curious about the new critters in the neighborhood rather than looking for a meal. She heaved a rock at the animal. It took off for the trees. She shouted and tossed a few more rocks to let it know she meant business.

After soothing the mare, Roni returned to the cabin, making sure the latch fastened securely behind her when she closed the door. She flicked on the lamp mounted on the wall. The bulb popped and went dark. There were no others. After removing her sneakers, she went to bed fully dressed, shoes and jacket nearby in case the bear returned.

She observed the stars through the tiny window above the bed. The sliver of new moon wasn't enough to brighten the landscape. The high mountain meadow was as dark as the terrain of her heart.

Adam was relieved when dawn finally came. He doubted he'd slept an hour the entire night. After a quick shower and shave, he dressed and headed for the kitchen.

Trevor and his uncle sat at the table, coffee mugs in hand. He returned their greetings with a dour glance and barely audible hello.

"Pancakes and bacon in the oven," the cousin said.

Adam ate, put the dishes in the dishwasher and returned to the table with fresh coffee. "I'm going out today," he said. "I'm going to find her. With or without your help."

He cast a challenging glare at Trevor.

"She'll come in when she's ready," Nick informed him.

"Fine. I'll stay with her until she does."

Trevor raised his mug. "You won't find her." He took a drink, watching him over the rim of the thick cup.

Adam narrowed his eyes at the other man in warning. He'd had about all he could take of the Dalton clan. "Then tell me where she is."

"Give me one good reason."

Adam raised his hands and slowly formed them into fists. "How about I give you two of 'em?"

"Still not good enough." Trevor picked up a ranching magazine and started reading an article in it.

Adam turned his attention to the uncle. "You're the one who insisted on this marriage. You going to tell me where my wife—" He emphasized the last word "—is hiding?"

After a lengthy pause, the older man nodded. "Trevor, take Adam to the cabin."

"I don't think he deserves her."

"Perhaps not, but they are married," the uncle said.

"I don't think Roni wants him anymore."

"Why don't you let us work that out?" Adam demanded, fury making the pulse pound in his temples.

Trevor leaned forward and stared Adam straight in the eye. "Give me a good reason," he requested softly, "just one." He was deadly serious.

Silence buzzed in Adam's head like a hive of disturbed bees. Total honesty was the only way. "Because," he said in a low tone, "I don't think I can live without her. I know I don't want to have to try."

"Does that mean you love her? Think carefully before answering," Trev warned.

Adam found it was painful to overcome a lifetime of concealing his deepest feelings. It left a man raw and open to the machinations of others. As he hesitated, he saw Trevor's expression harden. He forced air into his lungs and murmured the fateful words, "Yeah, I love her."

Trevor stood. "What are we waiting for? Let's get on the trail."

Uncle Nick halted them with a raised hand. "Don't rush at her like a bull on a rampage," he advised. "Maybe you shouldn't say anything at first. Just be there."

"Good idea," Trev agreed. "Roni never has been able to hold a grudge. She always comes around in the end, but it may take a day or two before she talks to you. With women, you have to go slow, play it by ear and all that."

Adam noted the amusement in the elder Dalton's eyes at the words of wisdom from his nephew. He wondered when the usually lighthearted twin had gained so much knowledge about the female of the species. "Right," he said wryly.

"You two going to jaw all day?" Uncle Nick asked.

Adam followed Roni's cousin to the paddock beside the stable. When he called, the gelding came to him at once, eager for an outing. He hoped his errant wife would be as welcoming.

Chapter Thirteen

Roni dragged the saplings to the corral and nailed them into place. She checked the rails and decided they were sturdy enough to hold the mare. During the night the agitated horse had broken through the temporary repair.

Returning to the cabin, she stored the hammer and tin can of nails on the shelf, looked through the supplies and finally spread peanut butter on some crackers that were stale but edible after being there for the winter.

Each season the twins made sure the place was stocked as a shelter in case hunters or hikers got lost. She was glad of that as she polished off the midday meal with dried apricots and raisins, then water from a spring behind the cabin.

The mare whinnied loudly.

Roni grabbed a walking stick she'd cut earlier and rushed outside. She stopped in total shock.

Instead of the lonely young bear, Adam rode into the clearing in front of the line shack, nodded to her and dismounted. Without a word, he unsaddled the gelding and put him in the corral with the other horse, who welcomed her stable mate with nudges and low whickers, then the two dashed around the corral in high spirits.

Roni frowned as Adam lifted his tack and headed for the cabin. He disappeared inside. She ran after him.

"What are you doing here?" she demanded, stopping inside the door.

He propped his stuff beside hers in the corner, then turned and gave her a thorough study with those penetrating gray eyes. "Enjoying the great outdoors."

"It's a good thing for you I didn't bring a gun," she informed him. "I thought the bear was back."

"What bear?"

She realized mentioning the bear was probably the wrong thing to do. It would arouse the protective instincts of a man like Adam. "A young one was nosing around last night. I ran him off. When I heard the mare whinny, I thought he'd come back."

"I'll check it out," Adam said with all the confidence of a superhero.

"Thanks. I feel much safer already." She stalked out of the cabin before she felt compelled to hit him with the stick or something equally drastic, then wondered why she was so upset.

Sitting on a stump, she soaked up the soothing

rays of the sun and searched for the calm center that anger and despair couldn't penetrate. It took a while to find it.

When Adam came outside, she ignored him as he checked the corral fence, found the bear tracks, then followed them into the woods. She refused to worry about him. An ex-husband wasn't her concern.

"I don't think he'll be back," Adam reported an hour later, startling her when he came around the side of the cabin. "He headed over the ridge into the next valley."

She nodded. "I yelled and threw rocks at him to teach him to stay away from people."

Adam smiled, making her heart wobble. "That would scare me," he said. He leaned against a pine tree, his hands in his pockets as if he hadn't a care in the world, and simply gazed at her.

"You'll get sap on your clothes," she warned.

He shrugged.

"Don't you have work to do in Boise?" she asked. "Shouldn't you be arresting some crooks or something?"

"That's done. As Geena mentioned in her message, we raided the office of the CFO at the telecommunications company and confiscated all the files. Also his computer and other records."

"Then you should be there."

"It's Sunday. It'll take a few days to catalog everything. The new agent is a whiz at that sort of thing. As long as you're here, this is where I want to be."

She blinked as sudden tears stung her eyes. "As you

can see, I'm fine. I don't need a baby-sitter. I would really like to be alone."

He shook his head. "You're my wife," he reminded her, a ghost of a smile playing about his mouth.

"Not for long," she said, forcing the truth from her lips. She leaped to her feet. "Seth can handle the details. I'll speak to him as soon as we return. You're right. We should leave now—"

"Not yet," he interrupted. He took a step closer. "We need to talk."

A fierce storm invaded her calm center, which had never been too reliable, anyway. She felt dangerously close to tears and refused to go all feminine and weepy in front of this strong, formidable man.

"Not now," she said, her voice a thread of sound in the vast quiet of the mountains.

"Okay. Whenever you're ready."

He pulled a dead limb into the clearing, went inside, returned with the hatchet and proceeded to chop the windfall into firewood and refill the box in the cabin. Later he went out with the fishing tackle the twins stored up there and returned before dark with three slender trout.

"Fresh meat," he said, looking pleased with himself.

She opened a can of bacon and cooked it, then used the grease to fry the fish. With a box of dried potato slices and a salad of miner's lettuce, dandelion greens and watercress from the creek bank, they shared a quiet meal.

While she washed the dishes, he dried and put them

away on the storage shelf. When she handed him the last tin plate, her fingers trembled.

"Don't be scared of me," he said.

"I'm not afraid of anybody." Well, maybe herself and her shaky emotions. She swallowed the knot that had lodged in her throat and wiped down the wooden table. Finished, she went outside to observe the twilight. The rain had come during the night, and the world was sparkling fresh.

"Fireflies," Adam said, sitting beside her on the rock stoop. "You don't see many of those anymore."

"No." Unable to come up with chitchat, she sat in miserable silence and wondered what the night would bring.

As the darkness deepened, she became acutely aware of the evening sounds—wind rustling the trees, insects playing their funny songs with wings or legs as instruments, frogs lustily croaking along the tiny stream.

A shiver cascaded down her back. She wrapped her arms across her chest to hold in the warmth. Adam put an arm around her shoulders and tucked her against his side.

"It gets cold when the sun goes down, doesn't it?" he murmured, his voice quiet, husky, alluring.

He rubbed her shoulder as if to warm her, but it only caused her breasts to bead into hard points.

"Don't," she whispered, unable to stand his kindness when she wanted so many other things.

"Don't what?" He clasped her shoulders between his hands when she would have pulled away. "Don't touch you? My willpower isn't that strong. Don't want you? I can't stop doing that, either."

She forced a cynical smile. "Sounds like a personal problem to me."

"Your uncle said I should go slow with you. As if that was possible," he murmured. "I think the time has come for truth between us." He stared into her eyes. "I want to continue the marriage."

She stood abruptly. Going to the corral, she leaned on the top rail and rubbed the mare's neck. "No," she said when Adam came over.

"Why not?"

Being a coward only made things harder. It was better to face the truth and get everything in the open. She faced him. "Because you'll regret it."

Emotion, fierce and unreadable, flickered through his eyes. "The only thing I regret is hurting you," he said softly.

He was a protective, caring person, but she was through running from the truth. Adam didn't love her. Yes, he could be tempted beyond control, but marriage was more than a passionate interlude. She understood that now.

"I'll survive." She managed a laugh to show him that she was fine. "I won't share passion at night and remorse in the morning. That breeds resentment. We'll end up hating each other. It's wiser to let go now and not torture ourselves with a marriage that won't work."

He was silent for a long, tense moment. "There's

one other thing," he murmured. "I've discovered that I'm in love with you. What do I do about that?"

She stood there, too stunned to move, while he went into the cabin. Brightness flared when he struck a match. The dancing flame became a steady light as he held the match to the wick of the oil lamp. The soft light beckoned her, enticing her to go inside and find out if what he'd said was true… Or was he saying that because he felt she was his responsibility now?

Confused longing banged around her insides, sending odd shafts of pain through her. She tried to figure out what his words really meant, but they made no sense, none at all.

Finally she went inside and closed the door against the mountain air. Adam built a fire in the stove and made them each a cup of hot chocolate with powdered milk and cocoa.

"Why did you say that?" she asked.

He handed her a cup. "Because it's true."

"You don't want a wife. You said so."

When she took a seat at one side of the table, he sat opposite her. He sampled the chocolate, then set the cup down, his eyes searching her face.

"I didn't know then how hard it would be to give you up. Once we started living together…in the same house," he corrected, "then I could no longer fool myself. I think I've loved you for a long time."

"Last year I thought we were destined to share a great love, but now…now I find that hard to believe."

"I know."

"You didn't want the marriage."

"I was stupid."

The regret was in his eyes again. That cold, calm center warmed up a bit. "It would be foolish to confuse desire with more lasting feelings," she told him.

"I'm not." He hesitated. "Have you decided passion is all you feel for me?"

Her heart felt very exposed as she shook her head. His smile was sudden, a gift when she wasn't expecting it. A light blazed in his eyes, but his expression was solemn.

"Okay, let's see where we are," he suggested. "One, I love you. Two, you love me." He paused.

She couldn't speak.

A flicker of doubt appeared on his handsome face. "I need to hear it, Little Bits. If it's true, I need the words. I know I don't deserve your love, but I need it."

You can run...

Once she would have said them proudly, but now the words were hard, so hard, to say. "I do," she said raggedly. "I do love you."

He released a held breath. "Let's start over," he told her. "Tonight. This moment. Our marriage begins now. No regrets. No concealing how we feel. Okay?"

Her heart tap-danced around her rib cage. "Okay." She took a drink from the steaming mug and wondered what came next. Was this to be their real wedding night?

"Roni?"

"Yes?"

"I think I have to kiss you. It'll probably lead to other things," he warned. "If you're not ready, speak now."

Regret pinged through her like a faint echo from a distant valley. "I don't have my pretty nightgown. It was for our wedding night."

"I know." He gave her the sweetest, sexiest smile on the continent. "I remember what you look like in it. We can pretend you're wearing it."

She glanced down at her jeans and shirt. Unexpected laughter bubbled in her. "Yeah, right."

He smiled, came around the table and scooped her into his arms. "Pretend I'm taking it off you," he suggested huskily as he pushed the shirt off her shoulders. The jeans followed. "Pretend this is our bed at the cottage," he said as he stood her beside the cot.

He stroked her thighs, then hooked his thumbs in the waistband of her thong. He easily disposed of it and her bra. When he kissed her breasts she wondered if she would get bigger there when she had a child.

"Shall I get a belly button ring to confirm our bond?" he asked, laying her on the cot and sitting beside her. He fingered the cross.

"No." She touched the wedding band on his hand, then on her own. "We've already exchanged tokens of our pledge."

"So we have," he said huskily. "And given our word of honor. I won't break my word."

She looked into his eyes and realized he was asking

for her word, too, and more—that she believe in him. Life had taken so much away from him. It was time he got something back.

"Neither will I," she told him. "My love is as enduring as the mountains. I will always love you."

He kissed her deeply, completely. "Once upon a time, there was a man, a lonely man, and a woman—"

"She was lonely, too."

Adam smiled at his beautiful wife. Her eyes were like the sun, shining with love for him, all for him. "He thought they could never be together because she lived on the morning side of the mountain and he lived in the twilight of the valley far below."

"But they fell in love," she said. "From the first moment they met."

He realized it was true. The attraction had been there from the first. "But he wasn't sure it was love."

She smiled and his heart exploded. "I was."

"Yeah," he agreed, running a hand down the smooth torso of his pocket-size Venus.

His wife.

His love.

"So they married, but there were complications. They worked through them." Then he proceeded with the rest of the fantasy, which turned out to be real…very, very real, as she tugged at his clothing until it was out of the way and he lay beside her on the narrow cot.

He held still when she snuggled close, then rested

one leg over his. Her arm crept across his chest as he ran a hand down her smooth flesh.

The wind moaned and whistled around the eaves of the cabin. It changed to a higher piping note, as if laughing at the foibles of the humans inside.

Roni moved again, pushing her nose against his neck as she cuddled closer. Her hand swept down his chest, then stopped at the juncture of his thighs. His lungs stopped working. A gasp was torn from him as she stroked him intimately. Then he couldn't move or speak at all as she explored him thoroughly.

When her lips moved against his neck, he managed to suck in a breath. "I won't last long if you keep this up," he warned, kissing her temple.

She laughed. "Don't you dare leave me behind."

He lifted his head. "I won't. I never will." It was his pledge to her. "I'll always be here for you."

Caressing his cheek, she whispered, "I believe you."

When she pressed, he opened his thighs and let her leg rest between his. She moved against him like a kitten, and sinuous delight poured through his veins.

Roni loved the heat between them. Lying against his strong, very masculine body, she wanted to explore every part of him and every bit of the passion between them.

Her nipples contracted into points that begged for his touch. Her skin seemed to have developed nerve endings she didn't know about. She felt him in every cell of her body.

"Make love to me," she murmured.

The world spun as he turned them, catching her hands and holding them against the mattress while he loomed above her like a god, firelight casting his body in gold and bronze.

Adam took her mouth in a kiss that burned right down to the very center of his soul. The bliss was almost too great. Then there was only the scent of her, the feel of her, the sweetness of her kisses as she responded wildly, willingly to his touch.

"Come to me," she urged, licking and sucking along his collarbone in a way that sent ripples of fire down his skin.

"Not yet. There's more I want to do."

He eased away from her and the sensuous stroking of her body, then kissed her throat, along her breastbone and over to each tantalizing little bud sitting atop her small, perfect breasts.

"I've never been very big," she whispered as if in apology, her fingers twining in his hair. "Maybe I should see about implants."

She laughed and he heard the self-conscious note in it and was surprised. Raising himself on both arms, he gazed at her chest, then into her eyes. "You can't improve on perfection," he told her.

Her lips trembled ever so slightly before she smiled. "That's the nicest thing anyone has ever said to me."

"It's the truth," he said huskily.

He laved the tiny peaks with his tongue, then suckled at each one in turn until she squirmed beneath him like a playful kitten demanding more…and more…

"Patience," he said, panting. "I'll give you every-thing…everything that I can."

"All of you," she said. "All of me."

It was what he wanted, too. He closed his eyes as he moved past her slender waist, then explored her belly button until he made her laugh and writhe against him.

Inhaling the sweet fragrance of her skin, he kissed a meandering path downward, across from hipbone to hipbone, then pressed his lips to the gentle curve of her Venus mound. He heard her sigh shakily.

Raising his head, he gazed into her eyes and found only love, excitement and curiosity there. He smiled at her, knowing this was still new to her and that she was willing to follow wherever he led, that she trusted him.

The greatest tenderness of his life seeped through him, all toward this woman…this woman, his wife.

Closing his eyes once more, he did something he'd thought would only happen in his dreams. He tasted her, slowly savoring the flavor, the delicate nuances, the honeyed nectar of her response to his caresses.

He slipped his hands under her, needing to give this pleasure to her, for her to know the same bliss that she gave to him.

"Adam?" she said.

"Yes, baby?"

"I think…I think…you must come to me."

"Not yet. Not until you come apart in my hands."

She gasped as he carefully increased the pressure of his mouth, then she stopped breathing entirely.

Guided by her little cries and the tightening of her thighs, he willed himself not to fly into pieces as he felt the tremors rush through her, softly at first, then fast and strong as the climax rolled over her slender form.

"In me," she urged. "Adam, now!"

He pushed himself over her. She guided him home. He gathered her close as he slid into the smooth silkiness of her. She was like hot whipped cream inside. He wanted to stay there forever.

But nature had another design. Her movements, the way she rose to meet each thrust, were his undoing. Unable to think beyond this very second, he answered her chaotic demands and moved deeply, rhythmically in her.

Pleasure sent shafts of pure ecstasy to every particle of his being as she locked herself tightly to him. When she went still, he pressed as deeply as he could, felt the throbbing release reverberate through her and gave in to the needs of his own body.

Experiencing something savage and possessive, yet tender and filled with wonder, he rolled to the side as soon as he could move, keeping her close, knowing he would fight whole armies to keep her there. Holding her, his world coalesced into one perfect whole. He was complete.

"I love you," he said a long time later, satisfied in heart, body and soul as they rested from the strenuous joy of their lovemaking.

"I knew you did," she said sleepily. "From the first moment we met, it was only a matter of time."

He raised his eyebrows in amusement. Her confidence had returned, that innate Dalton belief in the world and their place in it. He wouldn't have it any other way.

"Yeah?" he challenged just to hear her response.

"Women know these things," she told him sincerely. "Adam?"

"Mmm?" He nibbled at the corner of her mouth.

"Someday, would you play your guitar for me?"

He thought of his parents, of sitting on the porch in the summer twilight and listening to his father strum love songs to his mother. "It would be an honor," he whispered.

Trevor sauntered out of the stable when Roni and Adam appeared the next morning. "I'll take care of the horses," he told them. "So. Are you two sticking with the marriage or not?"

"Sticking," Adam answered.

Roni let her husband lift her down and handed the reins over to her cousin. "Did you tell him where I was?"

Trev nodded and held up both hands in surrender. "Hey, Uncle Nick said I had to."

Adam dropped an arm over her shoulders. "A wise man, your uncle," he said.

"He's been up since dawn, waiting for word from you two," the twin told them. "You'd better go in before he has another spell with his heart."

Roni smiled at Adam as they walked across the grass

to the front porch of the ranch house. "We're in for a lot of teasing from the family for being blind to what they will claim they saw all the time. Do you mind?"

Adam looked into her blue-as-a-cornflower eyes. The glow in those depths made him feel humble and very lucky. He knew he would do whatever it took to preserve the love and trust this woman had in him. If he ever worried about her safety because of his job, he had a whole gang of Dalton relatives he could call upon to help guard her.

He chuckled.

"What?" she asked, stopping at the door.

"I wasn't too sure about your cousin bringing my sister to a place named after seven devils, but it turned out to be a lucky break for both of us. I wouldn't trade you for an angel straight from heaven."

"Are you implying I'm a devil?" she demanded, trying to look indignant.

"Well, if the pitchfork fits…"

Smiling they stole a quick kiss, then went inside to greet the patriarch of the devilish bunch.

Uncle Nick grabbed them both in a big hug. "I knew I was right," he said, looking from one smiling face to the other. "It was as obvious as the nose on your face that you two were meant for each other."

Listening to Roni's warm laughter, Adam realized the love had been there all the time if he'd been brave enough to look for it. He suddenly hoped they would have a child soon. Their own little part devil, part angel. Their pledge to the future. Maybe they would have twins.

Double trouble. Double love.

He glanced at Roni. Triple love, he amended.

He smiled, thinking of it. Life didn't get any better than this.

* * * * *

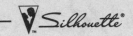

SPECIAL EDITION™

Coming in November to
Silhouette Special Edition
The fifth book in the exciting continuity

DARK SECRETS. OLD LIES. NEW LOVES.

THE MARRIAGE ACT

(Silhouette Special Edition #1646)

by

Elissa Ambrose

Plain-Jane accountant Linda Mailer had never done anything shocking in her life—until she had a one-night stand with a sexy detective and found herself pregnant! *Then* she discovered that her anonymous Romeo was none other than Tyler Carlton, the man spearheading the investigation of her beleaguered boss, Walter Parks. Tyler wanted to give his child a real family, and convinced Linda to marry him. Their passion sparked in close quarters, but Linda was wary of Tyler's motives and afraid of losing her heart. Was he using her to get to Walter—or had they found the true love they'd both longed for?

Available at your favorite retail outlet.

Visit Silhouette Books at www.eHarlequin.com   SSETMA

SILHOUETTE *Romance*

Don't miss

DADDY IN THE MAKING
by Sharon De Vita

Silhouette Romance #1743

A daddy is all six-year-old Emma DiRosa wants.
And when handsome Michael Gallagher gets
snowbound with the little girl and her single
mother Angela, Emma thinks she's found
the perfect candidate. Now, she just needs
to get Angela and Michael to realize
what was meant to be!

Available November 2004

Visit Silhouette Books at www.eHarlequin.com

SRDITM

SILHOUETTE *Romance*®

Welcome a brand-new voice to Silhouette Romance!
Nancy Lavo
will tickle your funny bone in

A WHIRLWIND...MAKEOVER

Silhouette Romance #1745

When it came to image, Maddie Sinclair knew how to remake everyone's but her own—until photographer Dan Willis convinced her she was a rare and true beauty. But once he'd transformed this duckling into a swan, could the armor around his heart withstand the woman she'd become?

On sale November 2004!

Only from Silhouette Books!

Visit Silhouette Books at www.eHarlequin.com   SRAWM

If you enjoyed what you just read,
then we've got an offer you can't resist!

Take 2 bestselling
love stories FREE!
Plus get a FREE surprise gift!

Clip this page and mail it to Silhouette Reader Service™

IN U.S.A.	**IN CANADA**
3010 Walden Ave.	P.O. Box 609
P.O. Box 1867	Fort Erie, Ontario
Buffalo, N.Y. 14240-1867	L2A 5X3

YES! Please send me 2 free Silhouette Special Edition® novels and my free surprise gift. After receiving them, if I don't wish to receive anymore, I can return the shipping statement marked cancel. If I don't cancel, I will receive 6 brand-new novels every month, before they're available in stores! In the U.S.A., bill me at the bargain price of $4.24 plus 25¢ shipping and handling per book and applicable sales tax, if any*. In Canada, bill me at the bargain price of $4.99 plus 25¢ shipping and handling per book and applicable taxes**. That's the complete price and a savings of at least 10% off the cover prices—what a great deal! I understand that accepting the 2 free books and gift places me under no obligation ever to buy any books. I can always return a shipment and cancel at any time. Even if I never buy another book from Silhouette, the 2 free books and gift are mine to keep forever.

235 SDN DZ9D
335 SDN DZ9E

Name	(PLEASE PRINT)
Address	Apt.#
City	State/Prov.	Zip/Postal Code

Not valid to current Silhouette Special Edition® subscribers.

Want to try two free books from another series?
Call 1-800-873-8635 or visit www.morefreebooks.com.

* Terms and prices subject to change without notice. Sales tax applicable in N.Y.
** Canadian residents will be charged applicable provincial taxes and GST.
All orders subject to approval. Offer limited to one per household.
® are registered trademarks owned and used by the trademark owner and or its licensee.

SPED04R   ©2004 Harlequin Enterprises Limited

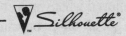

SPECIAL EDITION™

presents

an emotional debut

THE WAY TO A WOMAN'S HEART

(SSE #1650, available November 2004)

by

Carol Voss

It had been two years since her husband's death in the line of duty, and Nan Kramer was still struggling to raise her children in peace. But when her son flirted with crime to impress his friends, family friend and local cop David Elliott came to the rescue. David had always believed that cops and families didn't mix, but he couldn't ignore the sparks of attraction that ignited whenever he was around Nan—and neither could she. Could they overcome the odds and find happiness together?

Don't miss this beautiful story—only from Silhouette Books!

Available at your favorite retail outlet.

Visit Silhouette Books at www.eHarlequin.com   SSEOFWTWH

eHARLEQUIN.com

The Ultimate Destination for Women's Fiction

The eHarlequin.com online community is *the* place to share opinions, thoughts and feelings!

- Joining the community is easy, fun and **FREE!**

- Connect with **other romance fans** on our message boards.

- Meet your **favorite authors** without leaving home!

- **Share opinions** on books, movies, celebrities…and *more!*

Here's what our members say:

"I love the friendly and helpful atmosphere filled with support and humor."
—Texanna (eHarlequin.com member)

"Is this the place for me, or what? There is nothing I love more than 'talking' books, especially with fellow readers who are reading the same ones I am."
—Jo Ann (eHarlequin.com member)

Join today by visiting
www.eHarlequin.com!

INTCOMM04R

SPECIAL EDITION™

presents

bestselling author

Susan Mallery's

next installment of

Watch how passions flare under the hot desert sun for these rogue sheiks!

THE SHEIK & THE PRINCESS BRIDE

(SSE #1647, available November 2004)

Flight instructor Billie Van Horn's sexy good looks and charming personality blew Prince Jefri away from the moment he met her. Their mutual love burned hot, but when the Prince was suddenly presented with an arranged marriage, Jefri found himself unable to love the woman he had or have the woman he loved. Could Jefri successfully trade tradition for true love?

Available at your favorite retail outlet.

Visit Silhouette Books at www.eHarlequin.com

SSETSATPB

SPECIAL EDITION

#1645 CARRERA'S BRIDE—Diana Palmer
Long, Tall Texans
Jacobsville sweetheart Delia Mason was swept up in a tidal wave of trouble while on a tropical island holiday getaway. Luckily for this vulnerable small-town girl, formidable casino tycoon Marcus Carrera swooped in to the rescue. Their mutual attraction sizzled from the start, but could this tempestuous duo survive the forces conspiring against them?

#1646 THE MARRIAGE ACT—Elissa Ambrose
The Parks Empire
Red-haired beauty Linda Mailer didn't want her unexpected pregnancy to tempt Tyler Dalton into a pity proposal. But the green-eyed cop convinced Linda that, at least for the child's sake, a temporary marriage was in order. Their loveless marriage was headed for wedded bliss when business suddenly got in the way of their pleasure....

#1647 THE SHEIK & THE PRINCESS BRIDE—
Susan Mallery
Desert Rogues
From the moment they met, flight instructor Billie Van Horn's sexy good looks and charming personality blew Prince Jefri away. Their mutual love burned hot, but when Jefri was suddenly presented with an arranged marriage, he found himself unable to love the woman he had—or have the woman he loved. Could Jefri successfully trade tradition for true love?

#1648 A BABY ON THE RANCH—Stella Bagwell
Men of the West
When Lonnie Corteen agreed to search for his best friend's long-lost sister, he found the beautiful Katherine McBride pregnant, alone and in no mood to have her heart trampled on again. But Lonnie wanted to reunite her family—and become a part of it.

#1649 WANTED: ONE FATHER—Penny Richards
Single dad Max Murdock needed a quiet place to write and a baby-sitter for his daughter. Zoe Barlow had a cabin to rent and needed some extra cash. What began as a perfect match blossomed into the perfect romance. But could this lead to one big perfect family?

#1650 THE WAY TO A WOMAN'S HEART—Carol A. Voss
Nan Kramer had lost one man in the line of fire and wasn't about to put herself and her three children through losing another. Family friend—and local deputy—David Elliot agreed that because of his high-risk job, he should remain unattached. Nonetheless, David had found his way into this woman's heart, and neither wanted to send him packing....

SSECNM1004